UNDER THE NEEDLE

K.M. RINGER

Kisy Kane Publishing LLC

Dedication

Pa

Thank you for being my hero.
Thank you for loving me for who I am.
Thank you for always protecting me.
While I hope you never read this because of the sex
scenes, I hope I make you proud.

Content Considerations

Explicit Sexual Content

Blood

Physical Violence

Gun Violence

Torture

Kidnapping

Physical and Mental Abuse

Death

If you or someone you know may be struggling with suicidal thoughts, you can call the U.S. National Suicide Prevention Lifeline by simply dialing 988 or the full phone number 800-273-TALK (8255) any time, day or night, or chat online. Crisis Text Line also provides free, 24/7, confidential support via text message to people in crisis when they dial 741741.

Chapter One

Cameron

As I sat in the chair, Jax worked her magic on my back with the tattoo machine. She designed the piece: a lion roaring into the ether with a superimposed rendering of my grandfather in one of his military uniforms. I had found the photo of him going through his things in the days after he died.

I saw Jax's portfolio on a picture app on my phone and knew instantly she was the one who had to do the piece to honor my grandfather. We talked for months, hashing out the details of the design. Before long, we weren't just talking about the tattoo anymore. We were talking about what we liked, didn't like, and some of our hopes for the future. I knew she was the daughter of Don McMally, one of the crime families who ran Millford, California, but she seemed so real and down to earth, and not like any mobster/mafia person I'd ever met.

I even asked her out for coffee once, and while she agreed, something came up with her family, so she had to cancel. We continued to talk through the app, even having a few video chats. There was a connection, but if I was being honest, I was a little apprehensive about asking her out on a formal date.

When I came in a couple months ago, she did the outline of the design and said she wanted to work on the shading over a few different sessions, based on the size of it. Jax had explained there were a number of places where swelling could affect the final result, and with a piece that held so much sentimental value to it, she wanted to do it right.

This was the final session, where she was finishing up the last of the shading and making any repairs to sections that hadn't healed right or where the ink lifted.

"Cam, if you don't stop tensing the muscles, it's going to fuck shit up."

"Yes, Jax," I muttered and tried not to concentrate on how she felt leaning over the top of me. There were a few times I could have sworn she pressed her lips to my back, but I tried not to think too much of it, or I'd be going through a session with a major hard on.

Shit.

I'd had it hard for this woman for almost six months. It wasn't that she was unapproachable. Hell, we'd been talking a few times a week for months. No. It was her three bodyguards who were always around. One of them always had their sights on her.

She lifted from me as she chastised back, "Don't *yes, Jax* me." Rolling my eyes, I felt her chuckle. "Seriously, we are almost done. Don't make me fuck up when we are so close."

My head turned to where two of the guards were, and with my voice low, I asked, "Is there any way for you to ditch them?"

She sighed, and I saw the pinch of her lips as she changed out from the black to white ink, reset the machine, and leaned back over my shoulder. I felt the bite of the needle, but the vibration sent a calming sensation straight down my spine. "Cam, considering who I am, you know they are under orders."

"They won't even let you have coffee? Lunch?"

"Not without being babysat," she said through gritted teeth. "Overprotective bastards." She let out a long breath as her thumb moved back and forth on my back before she whispered, "I want to spend time with you, Cam. Why do you think I stretched this piece out over four sessions? I could have finished this in two, but I'm moving slower, just so we can talk and spend some time together."

I hummed and turned my head so I wasn't facing the guards. One of them was trying to pay extra attention to our discussion, and I didn't really want him to read my lips. "So, are you willing to go on a proper date with me? You haven't been stringing me along or fucking with me?"

"Yes, Cam. I would very much like to go on a date with you, but... Well, Dad."

"You are in your mid-twenties. Shouldn't he trust your judgment by now?"

She chuckled. "He trusts my judgment on many things. It's the caliber of the men and women I date he doesn't trust. He also... Well, things are heating up with the Mastonis."

I took a deep breath and laid there with her working away. I was racking my brain, trying to find a way for us to go on a date together, but each thought was foiled with just how easily we would be found.

"So, do we just keep chatting online, or am I going to be able to see you again?"

She stood and came to crouch down in front of my face. "Let me make something clear, Cam." I raised an eyebrow at her as her bright green eyes met mine. "You matter a lot to me, okay? We *will* find a way."

"How, though? It's a tricky situation on a regular day, and if you and the Mastonis are fighting..."

Her voice lowered, and it was barely audible. "I don't think you understand."

"What don't I understand?"

She leaned close again, her eyes flicking to the door before she gave me a quick kiss. It was over before I could truly enjoy it, and I craved more of her soft lips. Everything about her pulled at me.

"See, you are going to want more tattoos, and no one else is touching this skin."

"Is that so?" I smirked.

Her hand trailed down my body, leaving goose bumps in its wake as she walked around until she was standing at my other shoulder. When she bent down, cleaning and spreading a thin layer of protectant on my back, she whispered, "Because you are mine."

My stomach tightened and I couldn't help the twitch of a smile that curved my lips. She tapped my shoulder, told me I could get up, and I met her gaze. "Making a claim on me, are you?"

When she crossed her arms under her boobs in a way that had them lifting, I concentrated on her green eyes. There was no way I was falling for that.

"You going to deny it?"

The thrill that went through me at her claiming me had my cock hardening for her. Fuck. I swallowed hard, but shook my head.

She muttered, "There are things we need to discuss if you really want to try this with me, Cam. Though, by the heat in those eyes of yours, I think you can handle it."

"The question is, Jax—" I looked her up and down, seeing the way her chest moved as her breathing increased. She was in a tank top, which showed off her fine line and dot half sleeves on both arms that flowed up into the right side of her neck to the insignia that solidified which family she belonged to. Her fitted jeans cradled her muscular legs, and the handle to her handgun was just barely showing out of the holster on the back side of her hip. She had recently redyed her short red-blonde hair to silver, and it was stunning on her. "Can *you* handle *me*?"

It was her turn to swallow hard, and I noticed how she sucked in the corner of her lip. She nodded, and then a voice broke through, breaking the spell we had on each other.

"Ms. McMally?" She blinked, and I looked over to where one of her bodyguards said, "Are you almost done?"

Her voice was a groan as she said, "Not even close." My lips twitched, but headed over to the mirror and took a look at the last of the shading she did. A well of emotion sat at the base of my throat as I looked at the perfect representation for my grandfather.

I hope I can make you proud, Pa.

Jax came over and carefully laid some second skin over the fresh ink. I closed my eyes at the feel of her fingers working over the area, smoothing the material out. Her gaze met mine in the mirror. When she lightly pressed her lips to my shoulder, I cherished the feel of them against my skin and when she pulled away, I let out a long breath.

"Ready, Cam?"

"No," I whispered, but my lips didn't really move. She turned toward her bodyguards and headed toward the front while I grabbed my t-shirt. Slipping it on, I made my way to the front where she was making out the receipt.

We had already discussed the price, and so I pulled out the cash, and her tip when I reached the counter. After handing her the cash, she separated out the amount to the shop before quickly pocketing the generous amount that I tipped her. She hadn't counted the balance, and I hoped she didn't until she got home.

"Talk soon, Jax." My eyes flicked to where one of the suits was moving into just behind her, and then I looked back at her face. "Thanks for all the hard work on this. It's fucking amazing."

Chapter Two

Jax

"Wʜᴀᴛ ᴡᴀs sᴏ ɪᴍᴘᴏʀᴛᴀɴᴛ?" I turned and glared at my bodyguards.

"We have orders to get you back to the compound immediately," Jesse said. He'd been one of my bodyguards the longest, and I groaned, which almost turned into a growl when Jarvis stood next me. He was about eight years older than me and was the classical, tall, dark and handsome with his chiseled jaw, dark hair, and bright blue eyes. He was the whole package and I hoped the girl he had been seeing was worthy of him. He was a good man, even if he was under orders to be my second shadow.

Jesse looked up at me. "Look, we aren't ignorant, and we try to turn a blind eye whenever you have an interest in someone, but right now isn't the time to get involved."

"Fuck off." I turned and went to clean up my equipment. The owner would be pissed if he came in the morning and saw this mess.

"Ms. McMally—" I whirled and glared at them. "Jax, he did say immediately."

I glared at each of them before I pulled my phone out and called my dad. "Hey, pumpkin."

"Dad, I need ten minutes before we move out. I just finished a session and need to clean up. Will you please not kill the boys for waiting ten minutes?" I stared down Jesse, Jarvis, and Booker.

"Pumpkin, there was an explosion at the docks. Your name was spray-painted on the walls."

Confusion filled me. "Why?"

"We'll talk about it more when you get here."

Turning back to the boys, I just growled, "Ten minutes."

"Jax..." Jarvis whined.

Spinning toward them I lifted a finger in his face. "Unless there is an active threat in the hear and now, on this property, I'm taking the few minutes to clean up."

Their eyes widened, and I watched as each of them consciously pinched their lips together.

Ten minutes later, I was closing up the shop and messaging the owner that I had to leave a little early. I knew there wouldn't be any problem. We lent him the money to open the place, so he was indebted to the family.

Once we were in the SUV and speeding home, I pulled out my favorite honey lotion and put a dime sized amount in my palm before massaging it into my hands. The cleaner always dried out my skin, and the massage on my hands after a session always helped loosen up the muscles and relax me. I'd been working on Cam for a couple hours non-stop, and my hand was tired from holding the machine. Leaning back as I worked in the lotion, I thought about Cameron. He was sexy as hell, and I couldn't deny the way my core tightened at the heat in his eyes when he looked at me.

Give him one chance to back out.

Throwing my lotion back into my bag, I pulled my phone out, opened the app on my phone and texted Cam.

Jax:

This is your one and only chance to back out.

If he wanted to call it off, I would do my best, but I was possessive and wouldn't let him go easily. I wanted Cameron Martinez. I wanted every muscle of his flexing against me as he fucked me hard. I wanted my fingers gripping his long, dark strands of hair. I wanted all the heat and lust in his brown eyes directed at me.

Cam:
And walk away from you? Fuck that. I'll take the challenges. Just let me know when and where we can meet up.

Sitting in the backseat of the SUV, I tapped my phone on my knee, trying to figure out how I was going to be able to see Cam again. Sure, we could video chat, but I wanted a relationship with him. Only being able to talk to him through calls would be too much like having a long-distance relationship, which felt completely ridiculous since we lived in the same city. A city my father and I held a pretty firm control on.

While Don Juarez was king and held two-thirds of Millford, we held a quarter of it, which left the other two players vying for a sliver of what was left. For whatever reason, the Mastonis were now attacking our warehouses on the riverfront. It was good territory to have, but it was more conducive to our runs of supplies than anything the Mastonis moved.

"WHY BLOW UP AN empty warehouse only to leave a cryptic message?" I asked as I studied my father, who was standing behind his desk in his office. He was greying, and the lines in his face were growing deeper, but no one would dare look at him and think him weak.

"I don't know."

Slowly, I ran my fingers over the computer screen, tracing the lettering on the wall that was exposed: Long Live Reina Jaqulina.

"I've always hated that name."

My Dad looked over at me. "Only once your mother started disrespecting you with it. You loved it until you were a teen. That's when we *both* learned what a piece she was." There was sadness in his eyes again.

"Dad, if you are going to apologize to me *again* for something you had absolutely no control over, I might shoot you."

He huffed a laugh. "There's my ruthless girl."

I gave him an even look, and he lifted his hands up in surrender. "Dad, I'm not sure how *that* comment was ruthless. I've also always been very level-headed in any fight, so I'm not sure why you would think I was ruthless."

"You did it to get your team out when you got backed against a wall... Slit three men's throat... leave a knife sticking out of another's chest..."

"Yeah, yeah, yeah. So, what are we going to do about this? Do we know that it was the Mastonis?"

He pointed to the computer screen, where the declaration that I must live forever was memorialized, and asked, "What do you see?"

Studying it for a long moment before I groaned. "Really? They had to dot the *i* in Reina with their emblem?" I never really understood it. It was a winged shield with a templar cross on it. Looking back at my father, I asked, "Why 'Long Live Reina Jaqulina'? And why use the Spanish spelling for queen? Why would they want me to rule if they want to take things over? I won't be doing anything different than you are now."

I knew it was a veiled threat against my father, but what were they going for?

"Think about it, Jax. If they take me out, that leaves you at the helm. Sure, Juarez would likely accept you, but there are ingrained issues with a man not being in charge. I'm willing to bet that in the next few days, Mastoni is going to push for you to marry his eldest, Dominic."

"Not going to happen," I said coldly.

"I know. You want the guy you were working on tonight." His smile was a little disarming.

"While I think I know the answer, *how*?"

My father turned toward me and pulled me into his arms. I wrapped mine around his waist and rested my head on his shoulder. He kissed my temple and said, "I know how insanely talented of an artist you are. I also know just how efficient you are with your time. You stretched that piece out. Worked a lot slower so you could spend time with him."

"That transparent, huh?"

He huffed a laugh. "You haven't tried this hard to hide how you feel about someone from us in a long time. He that important?"

I took a long, deep breath and smelled the bold sweetness of the tobacco in his pipe. "Yeah, he is."

"Do you think he's capable of handling this life?" He pulled me back to watch me as I gave him his answer.

"Dad, you know it's going to take a strong personality to keep me in line, and..." I sighed. "Cameron can be that person, but I need time to see if he is capable of it long term."

He was silent for a long while before he let out a deep breath. "I promise to give you room."

Chapter Three

Cameron

A Week Later

The box of the elevator was crowded with people who all wanted nothing better than to get home after a long day at work. As I exited the elevator and stepped into the lobby, a man in a dark suit with a newspaper in front of him stared at the people leaving. I wouldn't have thought much more of it, had his gaze not trailed me as I made my way across the opulent white and gold ground floor entrance of the building. Just before I got to the doors leading outside, I caught movement in the reflection of the street-side wall. It was there that I saw the man stand and head my way. I tried to shrug off the odd feeling it gave me, especially when he followed me to the parking lot, but after rolling my shoulders,

I made a right to meet up with Bailey and Jess for coffee. Out of the corner of my eye, I saw him pull out his phone and snap a few pictures.

Why was this guy giving me such weird vibes? It wasn't like he was doing anything super suspicious. Hell, maybe he was waiting for a ride from a friend or someone else who worked in the building. It could all be a coincidence, right?

A few minutes later, Bailey and I were walking toward the coffee shop at the end of the block, laughing and joking around. Bailey looked down at her phone, completely oblivious to whoever this guy was, and shook her head, snorting in giggles.

"What is it?"

"Oliver just asked what Melody's ring size was."

Jess showed up then and asked, "He asked you, too?"

My best friends since college instantly dove into a conversation about everything they would do for their respective weddings. I opened the door to the coffee shop for them, and the man who had been on my tail since the office building was now leaning on the corner of the building. He was trying to look like he was on his phone, but unfortunately, I could see his attention flicking towards the three of us.

Again, trying to ignore him, I asked the girls if they wanted their usual as they waved to one of the baristas behind the counter.

"Of course, and a lemon loaf, please." Jess said, heading to the table we usually sat at.

I looked to Bailey, who smiled. "Can you get a rice crispy treat, please?"

"Seriously?" I raised my eyebrows at her. "You hate rice crispy treats."

"I'm just craving one." She shrugged, and I went to place our orders.

When it was my turn, the barista smiled, "Hey, Cam. Medium iced coffee with vanilla cold foam, a medium iced lemon tea, a large iced chai tea, light water, and non-fat milk, and a—"

"That's it for drinks. No Melody today." I interrupted her, "But the girls would like a lemon loaf and a rice crispy treat."

Within a minute, the baristas had our order, and I headed over to the table. Once I sat down, I saw the man who had been following me was now sitting in the corner, typing away on his phone.

What the fuck is going on?

The girls were still chattering away about Melody and Oliver, which was sweet, because those two had been circling each other for what felt like forever. It was nice to see that they finally pulled their heads out of their asses.

When I turned my head to give the impression I was just looking around, the man in the corner looked at us for a moment too long. I knew he was focused on us, and this wasn't some coincidence. As carefully as I could, I moved my coffee cup, so it looked like my attention was on it, and took a photo of him. The girls continued to chatter away as I opened my text thread with Jax.

Cam:

Did you put someone on me?

Jax:

No. Why?

Cam:

There has been a guy in a dark suit on my ass since I left the office.

Before she could ask, I sent the photo of him over to her. A moment later, she sent a text back.

Jax:

Not one of my guys. Where are you?

Cam:

Burnt Bean Coffee shop down the corner from my office.

Jax:

Don't leave. I'll have Jarvis and Booker onsite soon.

Cam:

Ok

"Cam, what would you do if you were involved with someone who was in a, what did you call it Bailey, a grey area of work?" Jess asked.

"Well, I guess it depends on how serious it is."

Bailey shifted in her seat and picked at the rice crispy treat while taking a sip of her lemon tea. When she looked back at us, I lifted an eyebrow at her in question. Her eyes narrowed at Jess before she sighed. "Serious. At first it just started as sex. Damn good sex."

"Naturally." I said, sipping some of my chai. "And now you've grown attached?"

Taking hold of the rice crispy treat, she opened it, and started picking out small pieces. "He has. It isn't that I don't care for him, he's just much farther in the process than I am. We are committed to each other, have been for a month, because I *do* care for him a lot... But there is something else."

"Wait, you've been committed to this guy for a month, and you haven't told us?" I asked.

She winced, and then stared me down. "Like you haven't been holding out on your new relationship."

I rolled my eyes at her. "You all have known I've cared for her for months. It's not like my interactions with Jax are new information. The fact that our resident *will not commit to anyone* friend, is in a committed relationship and didn't tell us, *that* is news."

Jess's flat hand flew out in my direction, saying, "That. That right there."

"Alright, *fine*, I should have told you. I'm sorry. That isn't the problem. I care for him a lot, but..."

Jess's eyebrows pushed together in confusion and I suspected we mirrored each other, but we waited for her to spill the beans. When she didn't, it was Jess who whispered, "So, what is it?"

Her voice was soft as she looked between us. "I'm pregnant."

I just blinked in shock as Jess sat back in her chair. Jess looked at me and I saw the same hesitation in her eyes as I knew I had in mine. I would be thrilled if Jax got pregnant, but we are still so early in the relationship, that we haven't even had a chance to have sex yet. Bailey on the other hand... they were a multiple times a week couple. Would her mystery man stay by her? Does Bailey want to keep the child at all?

When Bailey didn't get a word out of either of us, she asked, "What are you thinking?"

"What is your plan?" Jess pipped up. "That will determine how the rest of this conversation goes."

She wasn't wrong. If she didn't want to keep it, then we would support her in that choice and help her through it. If she wanted to keep it, regardless of what her man wanted, that kid would have two aunts and an uncle ready to doat on it relentlessly.

Bailey's attention bounced between the two of us and she took a calming breath. Her shoulders dropped slightly, and some of the tension left her face. "I want to keep it. Regardless of how Jay wants to move forward, I want the baby. I've never really had a family of my own until you guys, and I've never thought I would have kids. But now that I have the potential to be a Mom, I want to be the one that mine couldn't be for me."

"That is what you want. What about him?" My voice was soft and careful. I wanted to make sure that what she did with the baby was her decision, not anyone else's.

"I haven't told him yet, but his response won't change my answer. I don't care so deeply for him only because I'm now carrying his child. I've felt myself falling more and more for him, even *before* I found out about the baby."

"Okay then." Movement outside caught my eye, and I saw Jarvis and Booker striding by the windows, into the coffee shop, and storming into the corner. Booker grabbed the man who had been following me by the neck and hauled him out. There were two more of Jax's men, who I didn't recognize, following behind them who walked in, took the man by the elbow, and assisted him outside, where they disappeared down the street.

Jarvis, however, turned around, and when he met my gaze, he took a step toward me, and then paused, his eyes focusing on something behind me. When I turned around, Bailey's eyes were wide as she stared at him. He came over, and knelt down before her, cradling her face. "Sugar, what are you doing here?"

Holy fuck! Jax's bodyguard is Bailey's Jay?

"I'm having coffee with Jess and Cam, like I always do. What are you... Are you working right now?"

His head moved up and down as he kissed her forehead. "Yes. Don't be scared."

She looked at me, and I took a deep breath and muttered, "Fuck, life just got a lot more interesting."

Jess, however, didn't understand what was going on. "Umm, Bailey, is this your Jay?"

She nodded. "Jess, Cam, this is Jay. Well, Jarvis, but he's my Jay."

Jarvis turned to Jess. "It's nice to meet you. Bailey talks about you three all the time. Where is Melody?"

"Probably with Oliver." Bailey was not so fidgety as Jarvis' thumbs moved gently along her shoulder.

Jarvis reached up and kissed her softly, and the way she melted into him had Jess and me smiling at each other. "Hey, Sugar. Considering all this, I might be late for our date tonight, okay?"

Her focus went to me and Jess, before looking back at him and nodding. "Yeah, okay."

He turned toward me. "I'm sure Jax will be in contact soon once we find out more. Thanks for the tip. See you soon." Then he got up and left.

I closed my eyes and tried to let out the rising aggravation by clenching and unclenching my hands. "I'm sorry that he's going to be late tonight, Bailey."

When I opened my eyes, Bailey was shaking her head. "It figures he's associated with your girl. He's kept it pretty quiet about who pays him, but that *would* explain the owl on his bicep. It makes sense now. As for your apology, you can stuff it. He's had to delay stuff before, so this isn't on you. Don't worry, we *will* have the discussion within the next twenty-four hours."

I still gave her an apologetic smile, but it was Jess who jumped in. "So... Wait. You mean to tell me that your mystery man," she looked at Bailey, "works for your girl?" She shifted her focus to me, her eyes wide in shock.

"Apparently." I couldn't help the giddiness that went through my body at Jess calling Jax my girl.

"All right then. Jarvis, have any cute friends he wants to hook me up with?"

"Male or female?" Bailey smirked at her.

Jess just shrugged at her. "Does it really matter?"

Chapter Four

Jax

When Cameron sent me a picture of the now unconscious man tied to a chair before me, I instantly recognized him as one of Mastoni's men. Like hell was I going to let Mastoni get away with putting a tail on Cam. *How did they even find out about him?* To anyone else, he was just a client. We had been so careful, but unfortunately, in my position, there was never going to be a case where someone didn't find out about who I was seeing. We hadn't even had the chance to go out in public yet.

"Jarvis, can you wake up our guest, please?" I pulled off my sweatshirt so that I was only in a tank top and my jeans, and went to the table that had a few of my favorite word extracting tools on it. Tossing my sweatshirt to the side, I ran my fingers over the hilt of a few of the knives as I heard Jarvis splash water on the man.

I took hold of one of the scalpels and turned toward Mr. Chester Tolerico, rolling the smooth, metallic handle between my fingers. The older man sputtered and twisted as he came back to consciousness, only to find his hands bound behind his back and attached to a chain against the back wall. His feet were attached to the legs of the metal chair he sat on in the middle of the concrete room that echoed with the clang of the chain. His long grey hair hung down in strands, knotted and matted, like he hadn't run a brush through it in months. When he raised his head to look at me, anger filled his features, and his breathing quickened before his head dropped back down to his chest.

Tipping my head to the side, I asked, "So, Mr. Tolerico, why was Mastoni having you follow Cameron Martinez?"

The man grunted and shook his head. Stepping up to him, I used the flat side of the scalpel to lift his head so he had to face me. His eyes were glossed over like he was high. Scoffing and letting go of his head, I looked to Jarvis. "What did you guys give him?"

"Nothing more than a nice welcoming hello across the head." He was shrugging, but there was a bit of a wild glint in his eye.

Turning back to the idiot, I sighed, went back to the table, tossing the scalpel in the corner of the room in frustration. The metal clang against the concrete echoed, and out of the corner of my eye, I saw the man flinch.

"It's amazing how people become desperate when their wives leave them. Though, from what I heard about you, Mr. Tolerico, you fucked your girlfriends and had her watch a few times while she was tied to the bed. Told her she was worthless, and that you would never touch her again." I scowled. "I would have left you, too." Grabbing one of the knives, I turned to face him. His head lifted and the rage in his eyes had me smirking. "To bad the woman you fucked saw you for what you were and came to us two months ago, asking for assistance in getting your wife out of there."

I knew torturing a made man wasn't going to be easy, but one thing all men in this business seemed to have in common was their egos. I'd get what I wanted if I kept bruising his ego and pushing on that festering wound.

Tolerico pulled on the chains, and Jarvis tsked at him. "It's really no use. Stronger men than you have been contained by that chain. You'd do better to try to wrap it around your neck then get out of it."

"You bitch!" Tolerico spat, seeming to come out of the daze he had been in previously.

"I am. I am." I stepped toward him and bent down so we were face to face. "When Mastoni asked you to stalk my boyfriend, what was the plan?"

Tolerico spat in my face. Sighing and wiping it from my cheek, I cut away his pants and shirt, not caring that I sliced his legs, arms, chest, and back in the process. Once the fabric was nothing but ribbons at his feet, I got up, and walked over to one of the flame torches and flicked it on. That was when Mr. Tolerico's eyes finally filled with fear.

I brought the flame in front of his face, waving it teasingly, knowing it was his weakness, before lifting an eyebrow at him.

"Fuck you, cunt!"

Shrugging, I lifted the torch to his hair and watched as it burned closer to the scalp. I pinched the flame before it reached the skin and met his gaze. "I'll burn every hair on your head if that's what it's going to take to get answers, Tolerico."

There was a flash of fear in his eyes, but then his gaze hardened. "Go to hell."

"I already have the slide built, so that's not a problem for me. I'm quite comfortable with where I'll be going when my time here is done."

Lifting the torch again to his head, I lit the ends of his hair on fire, and sat back to watch. He held my gaze for a moment as the flames quickly raced toward the scalp. It didn't take long before he was jerking his head around, hollering in pain as the strands frayed away, and the embers found his skin.

"Okay. Okay." He finally relented. At my signal, Jarvis tossed just enough water over his head to stop the flames.

He panted and groaned for a moment before I lifted the torch again and said, "I'm waiting."

"Mastoni asked me to follow the kid. I was told to report back with who he met with, if I overheard any conversations, and the content of anything I heard as well."

Moving the flame to his shoulder, he flinched as the flame danced along the fabric of his threadbare T-shirt. "What have you reported?"

He whimpered as he tried to be tough. "Fuck you."

Smiling, I lowered the flame toward his skin on his arms, holding it just close enough that the air filled with the smell of burning hair. The heat intensified as I leaned forward, and he screamed in pain. I shook my head. "Wrong answer." When the skin was an ugly ass red, I pulled back. "What was reported?"

"He's a boring ass fucker. All he's done for a week is go to work, and hang out with those three dumb bitches."

I pressed the tip of the torch to the back of his arm, and his scream echoed the room. My ears hurt with the pitch, but I didn't stop scorching his skin. There was sizzling, the putrid smell of burning flesh filled the air, and then silence as his head dropped when he passed out.

"Fucking weak ass bitch!" Growling in frustration, I flicked the flame off and pressed the red-hot end of it to his throat. His whole body twitched, and I looked at Jarvis, jerking my head for him to wake him back up.

I pulled the torch back, and made room for Jarvis. He broke open one of the smelling salt packs and put it under his nose. Tolerico jerked and sat up, groaning. Flicking the flame back on, I placed it at his feet, next to his clothes, so that they would start to burn. Taking a step back, I leaned on the table and looked back at Jarvis.

"Don't you have a date tonight?"

"I do." His fingers were tapping against the table, and he actually looked nervous.

"Why so nervous? You've been seeing her for a while, right? Bailey, one of Cam's friends?"

He nodded. "I have a feeling she's planning on telling me she's pregnant."

My eyes widened. "Really? How do you know?"

"She doesn't think I notice, but I've noticed how she isn't drinking coffee in the morning, or that she hasn't wanted to go to eat sushi in a month, or that she's been on an emotional rollercoaster, or the fact she's had morning sickness every day for several weeks now." He ran his hand through his hair. "She was drinking lemon ginger tea when I picked up this douche."

"And how do you know what she was drinking?"

"I could smell the lemon, and taste the ginger on her lips when I kissed her."

Jax nodded as she stared at our guest. Tolerico's clothes had caught at his feet, and the flame was crawling close to his skin. I wondered how long it would take for the heat to become unbearable. Tolerico was watching the flames and tried to wiggle his way from them, but he wasn't going anywhere. They all thought they could get away, but in the end, every single one of them failed.

Leaning back on the table, I rested my hands next to my hips and looked at Jarvis. "Do you want the kid?"

A bright smile crossed his face. "I know my life is complicated as fuck, but nothing would make me happier than to have a child with Bailey. I love her, Jax. I know that having her, a kid, and this life would be stressful as hell, but it would be worth it to have my own little family. To give her the family she's always wanted."

"Very well. You'll have it, if that is what *she* wants. I'll make arrangements so she'll be on the protected list."

"Thank you, ma'am."

I watched as our guests' feet began smoking and sizzling, his cries of pain getting louder and reverberated off the walls. I tilted my head to the side, watching the skin redden and bubble on his feet. "No problem. Just invite me to the wedding if there is one."

"Done deal."

"Now, I don't suppose our guest would like to inform us of what else I want to know." I shifted all my focus back on him, and lifted the torch to burn off all the hair on his legs slowly. "Before he turns into barbecued meat."

Drool and blood were draining from his mouth as he whimpered.

"Tell me what I need to know and I'll end the pain. It's really that simple."

I was flippant with the words, but the man's eyes rolled up to meet my gaze. They were full of pain and defiance as he spat, "Fuck you, bitch."

"This is boring. I will give it to you though. I can't imagine the pain you have been in. Oh, I have an idea!" Taking the torch, I moved it to his tighty whities, slowly, methodically burning them off. When I brought the flame closer to his balls, he violently moved away from the flame.

"Okay. Okay. Okay. I'll talk." When I pulled the torch further away from him, he took in several deep breaths. "Mastoni wanted him followed to find out his routine. Says he's going to make you pay, and that *she* promised you to his family. That someone needs to put you in line. That you will be a Mastoni even if he has to take your Cameron away from you."

Crouching down in front of him, I smiled, and there was a flicker of final relief that went through his eyes. I had insinuated that I would kill him if I got the answers I wanted, but I didn't say how quickly I would do so. Never breaking eye contact, I propped the torch up under the chair, so that the flame was heating the metal seat. Then I went and got two more, setting them up, so they were more focused just under his balls.

I went back to the table and sat down on top of it, pulling my legs up so that I was sitting cross-legged. Looking back to Jarvis, I watched him as he took out his knife and started cleaning his fingernails. Needing to raise my voice over the screaming and whimpering of our guest, I asked, "Do you want a boy or a girl? Or do you care either way?"

"Don't care, just as long as they look like Bailey. Don't wish my ugly mug on any of my kids."

I chuckled. Tolerico was thrashing in his seat, but it was bolted to the ground, so he wasn't going anywhere. The room stank of burned hair and as he moved around on the chair, what was left of his underwear ended up on the floor. I chuckled as he screamed.

Jarvis smiled at me and went over to stand behind him. "Sounds like the heat is getting a bit much for him." With an evil smile, he pressed down on his shoulders and held him from squirming.

Tolerico thrashed in place, but Jarvis held him firm. After a few minutes, burning skin filled the air, and we just smiled at him while he writhed on the chair.

It took a little time, but eventually, there was some sizzling as he screamed and his voice broke just as there was a loud popping sound, and blood gushed and bubbled from between his legs.

The smell filling the room was horrendous, but also had a pleasant barbeque smell to it. I figured that was probably enough, so quickly, I pulled the knife from my boot and plunged it into his neck. Twisting it, and yanking it out, his blood flowed freely down his body, but some of it splashed on me.

"Son of a bitch. Blood is so hard to get out of jeans."

Jarvis chuckled behind me. "No one knows better than you."

I whipped my head around and glared at him. "Don't start with the jokes. Call Jesse and Booker to come in to dispose of Mr. Tolerico. You have a woman to see."

He nodded, and as I opened the door to walk out, I turned back to him. "Oh, and Jarvis?" He raised an eyebrow at me. "Congrats on becoming a dad."

Then I walked out and let the door close with a clang. Maybe I could be as ruthless as my dad claimed I could be.

Chapter Five

Jax

It had been two weeks of talking to Cam on the phone, video chatting, and texting. It was frustrating as fucking hell not being able to see him more often, but he seemed to be understanding. He had even told me, "Baby, I realize that there are going to be stretches when you aren't going to be available. I have to be patient. Know you are worth the wait."

So, while I had a guy who was super understanding and willing to wait, I wasn't. I wanted to go to dinner, a movie, do something, *anything* normal, but there was just too much up in the air. What was worse was that we still hadn't heard anything from the Mastonis since they blew up our building at the docks. It was just radio silence.

Even after I killed his informant, there was nothing. Sitting at the desk in my office at the compound, I sighed. My thoughts had been bouncing between the Mastoni matter and Cam almost incessantly. I had even been in a meeting with my Alpha team when my mind had wandered to when he had brought me lunch a couple days ago at the shop, but he didn't dare come more often until things settled down.

In the meantime, the boys were still hovering, but they had let us eat lunch together at the shop with minimal oversight, which was more than appreciated. When we had finished, I pulled Cam into the back, down the stairs, and into one of the storage rooms, all under the guise of needing to get money from my wallet out of my nonexistent locker.

Once there, I had pushed him against the wall, and his hands immediately gripped the sides of my neck as he whirled me around, using his body to pin me instead. I was momentarily stunned, thinking I had the upper hand. I usually did in these situations.

Cam bent down and ran his nose along mine. Just when I thought he was going to kiss me, he stopped. His lips move against mine, his voice low and husky as he said, "You may be able to run the show in every aspect of your life, Jax, but with me, I'll be the one in control in the bedroom."

I whimpered as I felt my nipples harden and my knees go weak.

Holy shit, this man actually made me weak in the knees.

I stared into his brown eyes as he cocked a smile and raised an eyebrow. "Cam.... I'm not used to giving up control."

His focus bounced between my eyes. "Being the second to your father, I assumed that. You should learn to let some of that control go, though. Be able to just enjoy the experience. Let me ensure your..." He licked his lips, and my breath caught in my throat as he murmured, "pleasure."

"I've always had to provide it for both me and my partner." His eyes filled with the challenge as I said, "I've never been with someone who is wholly focused on me."

He kissed the edge of my lips. "Watching you come undone around me is going to be the best kind of satisfaction."

My fingers touched the skin of his stomach, and I hitched my breath at the ripped muscles under my fingers. I was suddenly pushing back on the urge to take over again. I wanted to let go. Wanted to let the man holding me ravage me and make me forget everything except for his touch. So, while I was a little scared, I forced that dominant side of me to sit back and give him the chance. I trusted him and, with that thought, felt myself relax into him.

Humming, he whispered, "Good girl."

I did whimper out loud at that, and he smirked before kissing me, softly at first, and when I didn't take over, his lips spread into a smile. Cam then started kissing me with a ferocity that had every thought leaving my head. My fingers slid down and wrapped around his belt, pulling him closer to me, and I felt just how hard he was against my stomach.

My breath caught as his cock pressed into me, and he chuckled. "Not right now, Jax. There are too many eyes on you."

I took a deep breath and said, with only a slight tease to my voice, "I could kill them."

"You could, but wouldn't that be more hassle than it's worth?"

"For you to have to fulfill that promise you just made? No hassle at all." My head turned to where I knew my shadows were probably on the other side of the door. "There would be a fallout, though, and I guess killing them *would* be a bad idea, at least until shit in this city settles down."

Cam pulled my face to look at him again, and he was smiling. "Babe, shit never settles down in your line of work."

"Good-looking and smart." I reached up on my toes and kissed him softly again. Man, I could not wait to see if he could live up to those bedroom promises.

He stepped back and swung the door open, to where two of my bodyguards were standing with their backs to the door at the base of the stairs.

"I hate you guys."

"We know, Ms. McMally,' Booker said, turning to face me, but I didn't miss the glint of amusement in his eyes when he said it.

I hadn't realized I was holding Cam's hand until we were in the main room, and Jarvis's eyes flicked to where they were joined and then back off into the distance.

"We will talk later," I said to Cam, who nodded and leaned over and kissed my cheek.

When the door to the shop closed, I simply said, "It goes without saying, but not a word. Yes, my father knows about him."

Jesse looked out the door and asked, "Do we need to assign someone to him?"

My lips tightened as the logistics went through my mind.

It was Booker, though, who tilted his head in recognition. "You're seriously thinking about it."

"I am."

"If he is *someone*, then we should." His voice was low and coming from my left, but I just watched out the window as Cam pulled out of the parking lot and onto the main street.

"He's willing to take me and all that I represent, but..." I ran my hand through my short hair and threaded my fingers over the shaved part on the back. I wasn't sure why I was hesitant. Mastoni had already sent Tolerico to follow him, and I wouldn't put it past Mastoni to put another.

"He's observant. Caught Tolerico."

Jesse reminded me, "True, but Jax, he's already been compromised. Mastoni knows of his existence."

"Not yet. I don't want to subject him to the constant shadow until we are further along in our relationship" With a pit in my stomach and a sigh, I headed over to my drawing table and started prepping for my next appointment.

God, I hope I don't regret this decision.

***

When I got home, I went straight to my office and dove into the paperwork I needed to complete. Hours later, the door to my office opened as my father pushed it open and came inside. "Get some sleep, pumpkin."

Lifting my gaze to him, I pushed the keyboard away, folded my hands in front of me, and leaned on my forearms. I hadn't felt like this for someone before, and to know that it was an outsider scared me to death.

"Dad?" He raised his eyebrows at me in question. "You inherited the business from Grandfather and grew up in this life, like I did." He looked confused, but nodded. "I know Mom didn't turn out to be the right person, but how did you know when to bring her into this life?"

"Is this about your tattoo guy?"

I nodded. "His name is Cameron."

Stepping fully into the room, he closed the door, came over to the desk, and leaned on the edge. He studied me for a long moment before he looked out the window and said, "I knew pretty quickly, and we had twenty good years. It wasn't until you were older that I realized… and then she lost her shit. I couldn't believe she went that wild when you came home with a scratch on your face. Not because you fought and defended yourself, but that you had a scratch on your cheek from the fight. I hate the fact she was so concerned about your looks and who you would marry. Since you were a toddler, there was no way you were going to be anything less than the strong, independent woman you are. I couldn't allow her to continue pushing you into the arms of men who would try to squelch that part of you. Parts of me still love her, but I love the version of her that she was when we were younger." He sighed. "Honestly, I think she came to resent this life."

"Not the money, though."

He shook his head and laughed. "No, she's always loved the money."

I nodded. We sat in silence as he stared out the window at the city that we helped oversee. Sure, Juarez may reign supreme, but we were close-knit allies and kept the money flowing. Nearly half of what filtered through our accounts actually went to him. We were his conduit.

"Go to bed, pumpkin. Talk to your partner and give them time."

Nodding, we headed out and he gave me a quick kiss on the cheek before I headed upstairs. Pulling my phone out, I messaged Cam.

Jax:

You able to hop on voice chat tonight?

Cam:

Give me five minutes to finish something up and I'll lock the door.

I chuckled quietly. A couple of times this week, we had been teasing each other, and just when I'd see him start to rub himself through his sweatpants, his damn roommates would come busting through the door.

Stopping by the bathroom, I took my makeup off then slipped into a tank top and sleep shorts. I was wiped out, but really wanted to see Cam before crashing for the night. Trying to sort out what in the hell the message was really about had only led us to a bunch of dead ends.

Throwing the covers back, I opened the drawer with all my favorite toys and pulled out a thrusting dildo with a clit stimulator. I also grabbed the lube and made quick work of slipping it into place.

My phone rang with the video call, and smiled as I grabbed the remote, and climbed into bed before answering.

Chapter Six

Jax

Cameron was sitting there naked as the day he was born, and I didn't know where to look first. The lust filled eyes, the cocky smile, rock hard abs, or what he was fisting at the bottom of the screen.

"Fuck. Now *that* is a hello."

"Hey baby." Cam stroked himself a couple of times, and I lowered my phone, propping it up in the sheets, and moved my shorts to the side so he could see that I was right there with him. "Turn it on."

Cam started stroking himself as I clicked the remote so that it was on low, sucking his bottom lip in as his eyes glazed over. Hooking my thumbs in my shorts, I lifted my hips and slipped them off, tossing them to the foot of the bed. The second I spread my legs for him, there was an unholy moan that came from the phone as I watched him squeeze the head of his cock harder.

Pressing the clit stimulator harder against me, I rolled my hips and smiled at him.

"Pull it out and let me see that pretty pussy of yours."

I lifted an eyebrow at him, but when he gave me a commanding look that clearly said, *I'm waiting*, I grabbed the base and pulled it out slightly. The shaft thrusted in and out of me with short, strong pulses. I stopped when it was at my entrance and let it pulse and stimulate the pleasure nerves there for a moment, making sure that Cam could see it moving in and out of me.

His hand moved faster as he watched, and I didn't fail to notice his breathing coming in quicker. Smiling at him as I tilted the toy and let it continue to work my clit. Pleasure rolled through me, knowing that Cam was watching me. Slowly, I lifted a hand so that I could play with my own breast and pinch my hardening nipples. The feeling had me moaning and moving my hips involuntarily. "Fuck, Cam."

"That's it, baby. Fuck yourself. Cum for me."

I had been so wound up, I shouldn't have been surprised that I got off that fast, but his command had the world narrowing on his voice as he continued telling me how beautiful I was as I came, and how he couldn't wait to be there to taste me and bury himself deep within me.

As I shoved the thumping dildo hard into my pussy, I pressed the clit stimulator against me again and moaned out his name as I came. For the first time in a long time, I had a few seconds of blissful silence, before I opened my eyes to see Cam throw his head back, moaning my name as he released into his hand.

I stared at him as we both tried to catch our breaths.

"Nothing like a quicky before bed." He smirked. "Sorry about that. Guess I needed that release as much as you."

"Don't apologize. I was right there with you." I clicked the button on the dildo to stop it, and slowly slid it from me.

"Damn, baby. You are sexy as hell."

Smiling softly at him, I thanked him and told him I'd be right back so that I could clean up. He did the same, and after a few minutes, we settled into a gentle conversation. We talked about his day at work, his friends, how apparently Jarvis is Cam's friend's boyfriend. We laughed at just how small of a world it was before we both started drifting off to sleep.

CHAPTER SEVEN

CAMERON

"Hey, Cameron!" I stopped and turned to see Melody running up toward me as I stepped into the parking lot. I had a meeting in just a couple of hours, and it been a rough day at the office, so I was going to grab a quick dinner before heading over. It was a bit of a fluke that we all ended up working for corporations that happened to have their buildings in the same lot. As Mel would say though, *coincidences mean connections.*

"Hey, Mel. What's going on? Missed you at coffee last couple weeks. Heard finally pulled your head from your ass and have been spending some time with Oliver lately. Things going good there?"

"Yeah, and don't be an ass about it." Her cheeks tinged with pink, and I smiled. They had been beating around the bush for a while now. "He finally asked me out, and it's been pretty nonstop."

I knew the feeling. I couldn't think of anyone other than Jax. "It can get like that."

"Heard you may have a new lady." Her eyebrows raised, and I shook my head at her.

"We've been talking for a few months, but a lot more lately."

Melody gave me an even look as Jessica and Bailey came through the archway to the building they worked in to met up with us. "And is it true that it's none other than the kickass tattoo artist at Needle Works, Jax McMally."

A sideways smile crossed my face, and I just stared at her back. It was Jessica, though, who asked, "She's a fucking badass. I've heard of some of the shit she has done for her father."

I shook my head. Of course, that was what they would latch onto. Not that the woman was beautiful, smart, and was running her own businesses at twenty-six years old. Could she kill you with one look? Yes. Yes, she could, but there was so much more to her than just the McMally legacy.

"Bailey told me, by the way. She called me after she talked to Jay, who apparently is your girl's body-guard?" Her eyebrows scrunched together and she looked confused.

Bailey smiled and was shaking her head as she said, "Apparently. Who would have known that the world was that small?"

I looked to Bailey. "So what was the outcome of that discussion?"

Her cheeks bloomed red. "Not that I'll give you all the details, but let's just say he is over-the-moon happy. He also said that he wanted to get married, but I told him to hold off on that."

"Are you worried he just wants to marry you because of the baby?"

She smiled and shook her head. "Nah, I know he loves me, and we are probably heading in that direction anyways, but I just truly committed to him, and now I'm pregnant. There are enough changes happening, I need to get fully comfortable with all this."

"Totally fair." Melody said, smiling brightly at her.

Jess's head tilted to the side and faced me. "Bring her to the party tomorrow night I'm having at the house."

"What? Aren't we getting too old for the college party days?"

Mel was shaking her head as Jessica and Bailey looked at each other and said in unison, "We are in our twenties, not dead!"

My phone rang in my hand, and when I looked at it, I hesitated for a moment.

"Just answer her call, Cam."

Shaking my head, I did and said, "Hey, baby."

Jax hummed before saying, "Hey."

She sounded tired. "Everything okay?" I held my finger up to the girls, and took a couple steps back to let me have some privacy.

"Yeah, just... needed to hear a comforting voice and talk to someone that I didn't have to yell at to do their fucking job." She let out a deep breath. There was a long silence on the line, but it didn't bother me. It was easy with her. Easier than it had been with anyone.

There was a knock on the other end of the line, and she growled, "What?"

There was some muffled talking in the background before she continued. "I told Greg to get it done. Why hasn't he?... No, make his ass do it." Then there was a click of a door shutting.

"Baby..." I drew out.

"Yes?"

"Tell me what you need." I asked.

"You. Here. As soon as you can. Just need you to hold me for a few minutes."

I looked down at my watch, and nibbled on my bottom lip. I could reschedule the meeting I had tonight to first thing in the morning and still be able to meet my deadlines. "Do I have permission to enter the compound?"

"Is anyone going to tell *me* I can't have my boyfriend here? Is that what you're asking?"

I huffed a laugh at her teasing tone, and ran my hand along the back of my neck. "So, you've told everyone there?" I couldn't hide the smile. If she claimed me with the team, that was something.

"Dad knows as well, so, yes. Also, there is a possibility you will meet my father when you get here. Is that a problem?"

"No, baby. It would be my honor."

The laugh that came from her was lighter. "You say that now."

"Jax, I've known who and what you are from the beginning. I knew that if we were going to get serious about this, there would come a day I would meet Don McMally. And yes, I fully expect him to pull out the metaphorical shotgun and start cleaning it.

Fuck, I'll be surprised if he doesn't just put a gun to my head and start drilling me about my intentions for his daughter."

She was full-on laughing now on the other end. "Thank you for that image."

"Let me reschedule my evening client. I'll be there in a half hour."

Her voice was quieter than I expected. "Thank you. See you soon."

I waited for her to hang up and then turned back to the girls. "I need to head out."

Melody smiled, and I could see how happy she was for me. She was the one who had been closest to me for the longest. There was a time that I thought we might be a thing, but after one night out, we decided that friendship was a better option for us. It was just too weird. "Jessica's house tomorrow at eight."

"No promises. I'm a maybe, and well, she's a larger variable for obvious reasons."

"Yeah, we understand. You got yourself a hot bad-die," Bailey said, slapping my shoulder. "Haven't seen you this happy in a long time."

"I am. She's pretty amazing."

With a big smile on her face, Jess asked, "Is she it? She the one?"

As a wedding planner, she was almost bouncing on her toes at the possibility. "I don't know. We've only been really together for a few weeks now."

"But she makes you happy."

I nodded. "Need to run. Gotta reschedule a client and then head out. Text you guys later."

"Later, Cam!"

Chapter Eight

Cameron

When I arrived at the Spanish style mansion behind solid stucco ten foot walls with an iron gate, the clean cut blond man in a suit took one look at me, nodded, and then the fence rolled away and waved me in. I had barely parked my car when one of Jax's bodyguards, Jesse, opened the door for me and said, "Mr. Martinez, please follow me."

"Okay," I muttered, a little nervous for what I was walking into, and stepped out of the car to follow him. His tailored grey suit highlighted his broad shoulders and muscles, and screamed expensive. The whole scene was something straight out of a movie. I walked up the stairs to the stucco, Spanish-style, two-story home that had ivy growing strategically up the sides. When the large solid wood doors with ironwork opened and I stepped inside, her father was standing in the center of the foyer, framed by two iron banisters with curved terra cotta steps, was a staircase to the second floor. The doors slammed behind me, shutting out the light that came through, and when the lock clicked, there were instantly three guns pointed at me.

I almost smiled at the fact that I had called it almost perfectly. Instead, I took a deep breath to calm the adrenaline that was coursing through my veins and met her father's dark gaze. "Don McMally. It's nice to formally meet you."

He had a full beard, dark hair, and dark green eyes. There was a twitch in the right eye, and I saw the left side of his mouth come up just the slightest amount, like he almost didn't expect me to stand my ground and was amused by it.

"Cameron Martinez. Twenty-eight years old, with a degree in engineering from San Jose State University. Was offered a job immediately upon graduation, lives with two roommates, and has a decent 401K for someone who isn't even thirty years old."

I huffed a laugh and crossed my arms. "That is correct, sir."

"The fact you have three guns pointed at your head doesn't seem to surprise you?" His voice was even, and I heard the intrigue in the cadence.

"I just walked into your home for the first time to see your daughter. This is pretty much *exactly* what I expected. Now, do you want to discuss my intentions, or is there something else you would like to talk about? She seemed pretty upset on the phone and asked that I come over as soon as I was able."

"Dad!" I heard her say from the right, but I didn't look at her. I continued to give my attention to Don McMally. I knew I had to earn some sort of respect from him right away if I didn't want him to make it more difficult to see Jax.

He turned to face her, lowering his gun before he holstered it, and smiled brightly at her. "Hi, pumpkin."

She rolled her eyes at him, turned toward me, and in a few long strides, crashed into my chest. Wrapping her up in my arms, I kissed the top of her head and just held her as my gaze stayed locked on her father.

He smiled again and just nodded before saying, "Just remember that if you hear anything in this house, no you didn't."

"Understood, sir."

Jax mumbled into my chest, "For fuck's sake, Dad. Go away."

Then we were alone. We just stood there for a long time, and after a few minutes of me rubbing her back. I felt the muscles relax. When she took a deep breath and looked up at me, I saw the relief in her eyes. There was something heavy there as well, and I realized this was the first time she was coming to me for comfort, but it wouldn't be the last. I also realized she might not be able to tell me anything about it. I kissed her forehead. "What's wrong?"

"Just stressed out." She melted a little further into me, and a small smile graced her lips. "I needed this."

A small smile pulled at the corner of my mouth. "Anytime, baby. Anytime."

Jax pulled away and took me by the hand, leading me up the stairs and down the hall to the third door. When we went inside, I couldn't help but smile. For all the Spanish influences that were in the house, this room had none of them except for the balcony outside the double doors on the opposite wall. The entire room was lined with black paneling, with silver and teal accents throughout. She led me over to the queen bed, kicked off her shoes, and pulled me down on top of the black comforter.

Rolling over, I wrapped my arms around her and kicked off my shoes so they were on the floor.

She let out a long breath and said, "I'm sorry for my dad."

I chuckled as her lips brushed against my chest, and her fingers worked to unbutton my shirt, before sliding her hand between the fabric and resting it on my chest just above my heart.

"Better?" I asked, and she hummed her agreement. We didn't say anything, but I felt her breathing smooth out, and before long, soft snores came from her. My body relaxed under her, and I wondered why she had been so panicked earlier. Why she was so worked up she would call like that. Now, though, she was curled up in my arms, asleep. I felt warmth spread through me at the comfort she gave me. This woman, who could destroy anything she wanted, was curled up against me and sleeping. She was quickly becoming someone I couldn't live without.

As I looked around the room, on the desk was a photo of me laid out on the tattoo table at Needle Works. My head was resting on one of my hands, and I was looking over at her with a small smile on my lips. My eyes narrowed, but I couldn't remember that picture being taken. Must have been one of her guards.

Her room was not anything like I had expected. The room wasn't dark and menacing, or an armory, or lack of any character. I'm not sure why I expected those things, but I did. No, her room, while dark, was still classically Jax. The teal and silver accents were elegant, detailed, somehow still warm. There were pictures of her and her father on the dresser, and I couldn't help but smile at one where he was throwing her up into the air and they were both smiling and giggling. She couldn't have been more than four years old, but the pure joy on their faces was so wholesome I just stared at the woman in my arms for probably twenty minutes before there was a knock on the door. When it opened, her father was standing there. Jax didn't so much as stir. When I lifted my eyebrow at him, he smiled back at me and leaned on the solid black dresser.

"Thank you." His voice was low as he nodded to where she was out like a light. I gave him a questioning look, not wanting to wake her. "She's been working long days, and I think her only bits of sanity are when she is with you or talking to you. Thank you for being her calm."

I rubbed my thumb on her hip as I whispered, "She's something else, sir. I don't want to hurt her, and I will do everything in my power to never do so."

He smiled. "You have a way with words, Mr. Martinez."

"I know there are ways I could, without ever having the intent to, and I don't want that."

He stared at the sleeping woman in my arms. Her fingers twitched against my skin as if she could sense his gaze on her, but she let out a soft snore again, and he said, "The fact she allowed you on this compound, Mr. Martinez, means she believes you are worth it. We've talked about you. I trust her judgment, and if she is able to fall asleep on you the way she has, then I am trusting her in your hands."

I swallowed thickly at the responsibility and threat in those words. "Thank you."

"Any security she may appoint on you stays, of course, but..." he trailed off, and I simply nodded in understanding. He watched her for another moment. "If you want food, the kitchen is downstairs, otherwise we won't bother the two of you for the rest of the evening."

He pushed off the dresser and softly closed the door behind him.

I felt my heart rate kick up at what just happened.

He just literally gave me the okay to date Jax.

I took a shaky breath as I processed the revelation, and Jax jolted awake. "What's wrong?" Her head was scanning the room, and I pulled her back closer to me.

"Nothing, baby." I let out a long breath.

"Your heart rate picked up. Your breathing hitched. Why?"

Wrapping my arms around her, and held her tight for a moment before she got up and straddled my waist. "Seriously, Cam? Delayed response to what happened downstairs?"

I shook my head. "Again, I fully expected that. However, your father just walked in here and basically told me it was okay to date you. *That* was unexpected."

She turned to look at the door and shook her head. "I don't think he's ever given anyone permission to date me. The fact you didn't piss yourself when he met you at the door probably said more than any words you could have given him." When she turned to face me again, her eyes sparkled. "Was probably because you didn't piss yourself when you had three guns to your head."

"Wasn't the first time and likely won't be the last time I'll have a gun to my head if I'm with you, babe."

She stiffened and narrowed her eyes, where a fire was brewing. "What do you mean, wasn't the first?"

I shrugged and ran my hands over her thighs. "I've had my own run in with Mastoni's guys. Was young, and they wanted me to make some deliveries for them. My parents had just been laid off, and we were hurting for money. So, I did a few runs. Guns were pulled on more than a few deliveries. I got out of it as soon as my parents got back on their feet. Haven't looked back."

"I knew he used kids, but to hear he used you makes me even more upset. We really try to keep kids out of our shit, but just because I don't hear about it, doesn't mean that it doesn't happen." She sighed and looked at the door.

"He did say that if we wanted something to eat to head to the kitchen and, unless it was important, he would leave us alone." I gripped her hips, and she sucked in the corner of her bottom lip.

When her eyes met mine, they were filled with mischief. Rolling her so she was under me, I set-tled between her legs and pressed against her. The whimper she tried to hide was adorable. Bending down, I nipped at her lip and then sucked it in, running my tongue along the area. Pulling back a moment later, I asked, "I need to know what you are going to say if you need me to stop."

"A safeword?"

I nodded, and she thought for a moment. "Whiskey."

"Whiskey," I repeated, and she nodded as her fingers went to work removing my shirt. Once it was off, I lifted off her and stood beside the bed, looking down at her, studying the masterpiece before me.

She gave me a defiant look, trying to take back some of the control, and I lifted an eyebrow at her. "Remember what I said about the bedroom?"

Her eyes narrowed slightly. "Yes. I remember, but then why are you over there and not here making me do your bidding?"

"Patience, woman. I'm studying a piece of art. Deciding where I want to start worshiping." Taking a step toward her, I ran a finger along her jaw as she looked up at me through her lashes. Fuck, those green eyes were stunning as she stared at me with total trust in them.

She spread her legs, and I huffed a laugh. My finger ran down her throat, and I noted how she elongated it and her eyes rolled back. We'd discussed our likes and dislikes in the bedroom, so I knew where her lines were, but I was still plotting my course of action.

"Your pants," I ordered. "They are in the way. I want to have that delicious pussy in my mouth."

She was instantly moving without taking her eyes off me, sliding them off her ass, and tossing them to the floor.

Dropping to my knees, I demanded, "Bra and tank, too."

I pulled on her hips as soon as the bra launched into the air, and she flopped back on the bed. Her panties were now the only barrier to what my mouth watered for.

My name was a whispered plea as my hand circled her breasts, but I ignored the peaking nipples for the time being. When I caressed them, kissing her stomach, and slowly made my way to my first meal of the night, she murmured, "Please, don't stop. I need..."

I chuckled against as her words trailed off, and my jaw sat just at the crest of her deliciousness, pressing my chin down so that the swollen flesh would tease her clit.

"Please, Cam..."

The sound of her begging was like ambrosia for the gods. I loved the pleading in her voice. Her head was thrown back as her hips tried to move toward me. When my teeth pinched the fabric of her panties, her breathing hitched as she once again rolled her hips trying to find any connection. Slowly pulling them off her hips, I stopped only a second to inhale the musky scent of her, which caused my cock to twitch.

Sliding them down her long, muscular legs, I tossed them to the side and kissed the inside of her knees. The whimper that came from this woman was one of the sexiest things in the world, and as her legs widened to allow for my shoulders, I wrapped my arms around her hips.

When I reached her beautiful pussy, I slowly pressed the tip of my tongue between the folds of her, teasing her. Her hips moved, but my arms braced her in place. As I chuckled as she continued to beg for me to give her the attention that she needed, she raked her fingers through my hair and gripped tight, trying to force me to dive in.

"Baby, who is running this show?" I said against her skin. Just the sound of my voice caused the stomach muscles to tense, her thigh muscles to twitch, and as I looked up at her, I could see her pussy glistening.

"You."

"What do you say when you want me to stop?"

Her voice was breathy as she said, "Whiskey."

"Good girl," I hummed as I dove into her. My tongue explored every inch of her, and when I flicked her clit, her whole body twitched. I didn't slow or hesitate in my movements. I needed to taste her. Have her coat my face.

When I felt her getting close, I pulled away, nipping her inner thigh. She groaned in frustration, then looked down at me as I lightly blew on her exposed flesh.

"Please..."

I chuckled against her thigh as I drew a lazy circle with my tongue and then nipped at it.

"I love how you beg." There was no doubt she was frustrated. "Tell me what you want."

"Touch me, Cam, please."

My tongue roved over her luscious pink lips, savoring the taste of her before I flicked her clit. "I've been touching you, baby."

Jax panted as she said, "Please fuck me."

I dove back in, pressed two fingers to her entrance, and fucked her slowly. Licking and nipping at her clit, I continued by adding another finger, curling them against her G-spot. Her head flew back, grunting my name as she rolled her hips against my face. My dick pulsed, and pleasure ripped through me as I watched her.

I sucked in her clit, pressing it to the roof of my mouth, rolling my tongue against it at the same time my fingers hit that spot again. Jax's whole body stiffened as she gripped my hair tighter and groaned. I drank her up, cherishing every drop. When she had finally ridden out her pleasure, I stood and watched her in her bliss. Her gaze lifted to mine, and I licked my fingers clean.

Her chest was heaving, and knowing I could bring this strong woman that kind of pleasure only had my cock hardening more. As I slowly lowered my hand to my belt, her eyes trailed the motion, and in one quick movement, I slipped it off and tossed it to the floor, where it landed with a thunk. Her eyes focused on the bulge in my pants, and I smirked as I slowly released the button and lowered the zipper.

My cock pressed against the fabric of my boxers, and I hooked my thumbs into the sides of them and my jeans. Taking them off, I kicked them to the side as she sucked on that bottom lip and her attention slowly lifted again to hold mine.

"Fuck."

Chapter Nine

Jax

Cam was huge. Sure, I'd felt him against me at the shop, and, hell, I'd seen him on video chat, but to see just how large Cameron Martinez was in person was a completely different visual.

He gripped himself in his hand, and I watched as he stroked up and down his impressive shaft. "Fuck," I whispered.

Was I even going to be able to accommodate him, but his focus held mine, and I relaxed some. He crawled up my body, rocked his hips so that his cock ran between my pussy lips, and I reached up to wrap my arms around him. Kissing me softly, he nudged my entrance before he pushed in. The burn proved to me just how much bigger he was than everyone else I had ever been with.

When I let out a relaxing breath, he paused, giving me a questioning look. "You okay?"

Hesitantly, because I was, but said, "I'm... You're so much bigger. Can I—"

"I'll fit, baby. I promise." He held my gaze as he dragged out and slowly pushed back in, repeating the motion a few times before he was fully seated deep within me. My hips rolled of their own accord, and my pussy was already twitching in pleasure as he muttered, "See, look at you taking me so fucking perfectly."

Heat flowed through me at his words. He trailed kisses down my neck and collarbone as he slowly, but with purpose, fucked me.

No, this wasn't a fuck. There was too much emotion in his movements.

He pulled back, I studied his eyes. There was true emotion there. Just open, honest, *this is me.*

"Fuck, you are gripping me tight. It's amazing."

I was hanging on an emotional ledge with him. He was the only one who could calm me, and this... No one had given me this before.

"Cam... ," I said as my hips rolled to meet his. With each slam home, I was closer and closer to falling into orgasmic bliss. This man was ruining me in every possible way.

He cradled my cheek in his hand and ran his thumb across my bottom lip. Sucking it in, I teased it with my tongue, and he twitched as he buried himself harder. I pinched his thumb between my teeth and moaned. Smirking, Cameron took one of my knees and brought it to my ribs as he leaned down and groaned. "You like to fucking tease me like that?"

His thumb was still between my lips, so I sucked and swirled my tongue around the tip. He removed his thumb just before his lips slammed onto mine. His tongue caressed mine as I gasped when he pounded into me. Seconds away from cumming on his cock, I was trying to hold out.

Cam's tongue only increased the pleasure as he made love to my mouth, causing me to run my nails across his back. I swallowed the moan he gave me as he kissed me. When I repeated the motion, he reached down and tweaked my nipple. "Cum for me, baby."

He fucked me hard and fast while he pinched harder on my nipple, but I lost all sound and sight as he kissed along my neck and whispered my name in my ear. "You fucking feel amazing wrapped around my cock. Fuck, Jax. You're perfect."

"Cam!" I shouted, and then moaned as wave after wave of pleasure consumed me. His hips moved with mine, and I kissed his neck as he buried himself deep within me. The feel of his lips on my neck was hot as fucking hell as he kissed me. After getting his own breathing under control, he asked where the bathroom was.

"Door next to the mirror."

He was gone only a minute before he came back and cleaned me up. He went and dropped the towel in the clothes basket, then lifted the blankets and asked me to get in. Sliding in behind me, he wrapped his arm around my waist and kissed the back of my neck. I'd never felt so settled after sex. Never so complete.

His mouth was moving against my skin, but I couldn't make out what he was saying. If I wasn't exhausted, I would have asked. Only sleep was stronger, and I fell to its spell.

Chapter Ten

Cameron

I OPENED MY EYES to find Jax curled up into my chest, drawing lazy circles on my pecs. Her focus slowly trailed from where her finger was working, up my neck, and then up to my eyes.

"Hey."

"Hey." She smiled up at me. "Thank you."

"Whatever for, baby?"

She took a long breath and said, "For standing up before my father and not cowering. For caring about me. For coming into my life."

As she studied me, Jessica's question kept going through my mind. *Was she it for me?* Maybe, but we had only been together for a few weeks and had hardly been able to see each other in person. Sure, we had talked every night, had been for months, but...

"You're mine, Jax. I know it may be a weakness in your world, but I'll do anything for you. You may be the heir of a Don, but if anyone were to try to hurt you, I would be right with your father's men to get you back," I vowed.

She swallowed and lifted to kiss me softly. "I'll always keep you safe, Cam. I have a request, though."

"What's that?"

"Can we go get some food, please? I'm hungry."

Giving her a questioning look, I ran my thumb along her cheek. "Why would I keep you from eating? I know better than to let my woman get hangry."

That sassy smirk I loved so much appeared. "Well, you said you wanted to be in control in the bedroom. We *are* in the bedroom."

Kissing her forehead, I chuckled. "Baby, while I appreciate the attempt, I know that once sex is over, you are right back at the forefront." Kissing her softly again, I dropped my voice and muttered, "I'm so proud of you for letting go today."

Her arm tightened around me, and I felt her lips press on my throat. The gentleness of it squeezed at my heart. "Come on, let's get you some food."

Untangling herself from me, she bounced out of the bed, and we got dressed in comfortable silence.

After she used the bathroom, we stepped out into the hall and she pulled me to a stop.

Voices flowed up the stairway, and after a moment, she nodded before she led me downstairs as she explained, "Had to make sure Dad wasn't, well... ya'know business."

As we passed her father in the foyer, I simply nodded and let her pull me into the kitchen. Efficiently bouncing from one area of the room to another, she pulled out a pot, filling it with water, and set it to boil. Jax smirked as she pulled out a large box of pasta, and went to the freezer to pull out two bags of frozen pasta sauce and grabbed another pot on her way back to the stove. Winking at me, she dumped it on the counter.

"No jar sauce?" I smirked at her.

She whirled at me, and raised a finger pointing at me. "Not in this house. Every two weeks, I spend hours in this kitchen making my Nona's family recipe. She would roll over in her grave if she ever found us served store bought sauce."

"Your family name is Irish though, not Italian."

She turned back to the stove and went to work. "Poppa McMally was on a trip to Italy when he met Nona. Said it was love at first bite." She chuckled and

I couldn't help the smile that spread across my face. Reminded me of when I first saw her. "A year later, they moved to America, and he quickly created the family business. The rest is history."

"Who taught you to cook?"

She was putting the sauce together for the pasta when I saw the deep breath she took before she said, "My Nona. I was ten when she died, then my mother took over. Said if I was going to keep a husband of worth, I had to hold my weight in the kitchen, not my waist."

I didn't ask her to elaborate. Everyone knew that there had been a very ugly divorce between her parents. She continued to work on the pasta and then reached over to grab a couple of bowls, filling them for us. After placing them before me, she held a finger up. "Hold on one more minute."

Jax put her fingers between her lips and let out a three-note whistle that had about six guys flocking into the room, lining up, and gathering their pasta before leaving again. She smiled when her father walked through and gave her a kiss on the cheek. "Thank you."

"No problem, Dad."

He nodded and then we were alone again.

I was smiling at her when she turned around and slipped onto the barstool next to me. Picking up her fork, she twirled up some of her spaghetti and took a bite.

Shaking my head at her in awe, I said, "You are something else."

"I've lived here my whole life. Know how things are. I could tell by the way the men were standing and the fatigue in Dad's face that they hadn't stopped for dinner. I also know who he was standing there with, and that man is a wordy bastard. He can make a three-hour meeting out of something that could have been a two-sentence email."

After we ate a few more bites, she continued, "Mom taught me how to cook, how to anticipate the needs of the house, and so many other things."

She played with the noodles in her bowl for a minute, but then she looked out the window over the sink. "When I was ten or eleven, things changed with her. I don't know what it was exactly, but by the time I was twelve, she started using me as a way to gain favor, pity, or some kind of attention from other people. I had heard a rumor she was trying to promise marriage to the right person for the right benefits. Would always be like, 'Oh, *Jaqulina is so obedient, loving, and attentive to everyone's needs and wants,'* or *'Jaqulina will be quiet and malleable, and conform whatever your needs are,'* or *'Jaqulina will be able to produce many high-quality heirs for you.'* It was one thing to have her try to sell me off, but she pretended that wasn't what she was doing. It was even worse when she tried to take credit for my achievements. Everything I did was about how she fostered me into whatever it was that I was doing at the time."

My eyebrows pinched together in astonishment, and I couldn't believe her mother would treat her like that.

"Cam, I'm not telling you this for you to feel sorry for me. I am telling you so you can see how I got to be the person I am."

"I'm not feeling sorry for you. I'm trying to understand what was wrong with her that she didn't feel that she could let you just be a kid."

Jax shook her head and looked off through the doorway to the left. "Yeah, the straw that broke the camel's back was when I was at school and I got into a particularly bad fight. I'm my father's daughter. Fights weren't uncommon, but Dad and I had a deal—if someone swung first, I could finish it. Whether that was just disarming them, pinning them until they caved, we got in trouble, or whether I beat the shit out of them, he understood I would stop swinging once the opportunity arose. In this particular situation, the kid had a knife. He had sliced up my face and down my arm. I eventually had him incapacitated, sitting on his back with his hands pinned behind him with one hand and the knife in the other. As Doc stitched me up, Dad told me good job, but you know what my mother said?"

I shook my head.

Her voice went up an octave. "How *dare* you damage your face? What are people going to think of *me* now that it's marred?"

"Utter bullshit." I could not believe this woman. How could she treat her daughter like that?

"That was the night that my father went upstairs, packed her shit, calmly set it in the foyer, and told her to get out. When she wouldn't leave of her own accord, he literally tossed her out on her ass. Told her she could have the condo on the southside and he never wanted to see her again. If she tried to sell me off or claim me in any way, *she* would disappear."

I picked at my food and eventually pushed it away, leaving about a quarter of it left. When she took the bowl, she continued, "I heard a lot of what was happening through the media. Some of it was wrong, some of it turned out to be true. Dad really tried to keep me out of it. I'm pretty sure he pulled some strings, because he had a divorce decree with him named as the sole legal guardian of me within a week. My mother can't even claim me as her blood on any legal document, not even as an heir. Had her completely removed from everything."

I gave her an incredulous look. "He just did that? Why?"

She shrugged. "I agreed to it. I didn't want anything to do with her anymore. I wanted her out of my life. Still do. Certainly wouldn't throw a coffee on her if she were on fire. Those things are expensive, and she's not worth it. He sends her ten grand a month, just to keep her at bay, but I haven't seen or heard from her in over ten years. It's been great."

I couldn't imagine not having my parents in my life. Though they both loved and supported me in whatever it was I wanted to do. It wasn't like Jax didn't have a loving parent. It was clear as day when I saw her father look at her how much he loves and cherishes her. I was certain that if anyone harmed a hair on her head, he would burn the city for her.

We dished up a few quick-grab meals with the leftovers. It was nice to just do something domestic with her. We worked in silence as we wiped up the counters and washed the dishes before setting them on the rack to dry. It gave me time to absorb what she had told me about her parents. The grooming that her mother tried to do was horrendous. I'd read case studies about it, and it was one of those things that rarely had intervention. The fact that her father was able to was amazing.

When we were done, I looked up at the clock that hung over the doorway and sighed as I leaned against the counter. "I should head home."

She froze, turned, took three steps to stand in front of me, and fisted her hand in my shirt at my waist. "Or you could stay tonight."

I blinked. "Is that going to be a problem if I do?"

Jax leaned against me, and I wrapped my arms around her waist as she tilted her head back and looked at me. "I've claimed you, Cameron Martinez. Everyone on the compound, and that includes both Alpha and Beta teams, knows who you are to me and that you are allowed free access to the property." I lifted an eyebrow at her. "Notice that it was only my dad's guys who pulled guns on you and you had no problem getting past the gate?"

I stared at her in disbelief.

"I'm all-in with you, Cam." Lifting a finger and putting it in my face, she said, "Don't make me regret it."

"Wouldn't dream of it." Kissing her, I felt her melt into me.

She pulled back, went to the fridge and grabbed a couple of water bottles, tossing one of them to me. Just as I caught it in my hand, she smiled. "I don't think I'm tired enough to sleep. Think you could wear me out for bed?"

I lowered my head, looked at her through my eyebrows, and smirked. "Oh, you better run, baby. The only thing keeping me from fucking you on this counter is the respect I have for your father."

Jax lifted an eyebrow at me. "Respect or fear?"

"No reason it can't be both." I chuckled. "Now get your ass up stairs."

She turned and bolted. One of the house guards came in with a pile of bowls and smiled at me, jerking his head after her. I smiled and took off. At the top of the stairs, her door was open, but when I ran through it, she was there handing me my phone.

"Your phone is going off non-stop. You need all your attention on me while you fuck me to sleep."

Reaching out and gripping her chin between my thumb and forefinger, I pulled her to me and kissed her softly. I pulled back and sighed when I saw there were thirteen messages from the girls.

I looked over at Jax and sighed heavily as I settled back onto the bed. "Don't suppose you are free tomorrow night at eight to go to a party at my friend Jessica's house? They kind of want to meet you."

"You want me to meet your friends?" She looked a little surprised and searched my face for any hesitation.

"Why wouldn't I?"

"I'm Jax McMally."

"Yeah, and I'm Cameron Martinez." I went to stand before her and lifted her chin with a finger, "Baby, you aren't meeting them as the heir to the McMally legacy. You are meeting my best friends as the woman I care for."

She fidgeted with the front of my shirt again before meeting my gaze. "This would be Jessica, Bailey, and Melody?"

I smirked because, *of course*, she knew all their names. Probably had complete files on each of them with information spanning from birth to what they had for breakfast this morning.

"You've done your homework." I kissed her softly, so she knew I wasn't mad at her. "We've been friends since we were freshmen at San Jose State. I went on one date with Melody, but we realized halfway through that friendship was our only course of action. The other two, there was never anything."

"Do you think I'd be jealous?" There was a teasing smirk as she met my gaze, and it was adorable as hell.

"I would like to hope not, but figured I should tell you just in case. Previous girlfriends had issues with me staying friends with her, and that's a non-starter for me. She's been there for me when others haven't."

She smiled at me and reached up to kiss me softly. "I'm not worried. Appreciate you telling me, though."

I kissed her again and let it sit languidly on her lips. "I only want you. Only you, my precious Jax."

Her cheeks flushed. "Okay, and I'd love to meet your friends. I have a meeting at five, and it will take a few hours. Send me the address and I'll meet you there as soon as I can. Now, can you please take me to bed?"

His thumb rubbed against my bottom lip. "Anything you want."

Chapter Eleven

Jax

I looked at the clock for the tenth time. It was nine-thirty, and I had already texted Cam that I was running late. He had reassured me it was fine and that Jessica's parties typically went late into the night, but he understood if I wasn't able to make it.

The problem was I would much rather be there with him than sitting here listening to this cranky old man bitch about why his shipment was late. It was time to end this. I had a man to see, and this fucker had taken up enough of my time.

Cutting him off mid-sentence, I said, "Mr. Kalo, I understand your discourse, but I do have somewhere else I need to be, so we are done. I have given you my answer."

Leading him outside, I looked to my father, who nodded. However, as soon the door was shut, Greg came in with blond hair that looked as if it had been tossed in the wind and his breathing was labored, likely from running up the stairs from where his computer lab was. "Ma'am."

"What is it?" My stomach immediately dropped when I thought of Cam.

He handed me a sheet of paper, and when I read it, my heart stopped.

Reina Jaqulina,

Agree to marriage with Dominic Mastoni. If the agreement isn't legally binding by the end of the night, you will never see Cameron Martinez again.

Until then, he will be safe in our custody.

-Mastoni

Pulling my phone out, I called Cam. When I got his voicemail, I shouted for Jesse, Booker, and Jarvis. My eyes met Dad's, and he said, "We will relay what information we can from here. Send me the address of where you were going and we will work backwards. Check for where he may be. We will find him and bring him home."

Nodding, I headed out. James slid behind the wheel, and Booker, Jarvis, and I held on tight as he sped through the streets. I tried Cam's phone again, and this time a woman answered. "Hello, Ms. McMally."

It wasn't a voice I knew, but I asked, "Is Cam there? Can you please put him on the phone?"

"Umm..." She was quiet for a long minute, and then she said, "I don't see him. This is Melody, by the way. I last saw him stepping out the back door. Figured he was just waiting for you."

"I'll be there in less than two minutes. Meet me out front."

In a minute and a half, we pulled in front of the house and a tall brunette was standing there, holding out his phone. "Thanks, Melody."

I handed it to Jarvis, who headed back to the car. He would get information to Greg and help us out.

"Did you see anyone strange here?" I asked Melody as two blondes came outside.

"Melody?" They looked at me and blinked.

"Jessica. Bailey." They stared back in confusion. "Yes, I know your names. But right now, I really don't care about pleasantries. Where is Cam?"

I felt my voice crack just the slightest at his name, and their eyes softened. Bailey took a step toward me and asked, "He means that much to you?"

I nodded once.

They all looked at each other for a moment. "Okay, what do you need from us?"

"A guest list. Or anyone you can remember being here. Did you see anyone that may have had a winged shield tattooed on their neck?"

My phone vibrated in my hand as I looked at Melody. "Yeah. A blonde was hitting on us and his hair kept moving to uncover it. He took off about thirty minutes ago."

Nodding, I saw a message from George, but then my phone rang immediately.

I answered, "Give me good news." I put my hand on my hip and looked at his friends. There was worry in each of their eyes, and Jessica was shifting from foot to foot.

"Needle Works. Camera picked up a Mastoni SUV parked in the shadows, unloading someone."

Smirking, I looked at the girls and said, "I'll get him back." They nodded, and I turned for the car.

Greg's voice came through my phone again. "Alpha will meet you there."

"We are twenty out."

"James is driving?"

"Yup," I said as James brought the engine to life, and I shut the door.

The wheels spun out as James launched the SUV into action.

Chapter Twelve

Cameron

Fuck, my head hurts. It was pounding like I had just spent days at a rave. Blinking several times to clear my vision, I slowly lifted it to see a woman sitting in a chair in the corner, but I couldn't see her face through the shadows. Next to her, the bulb was illuminating a man I had seen on the news for years. His thick black beard, piercing blue eyes, and broad chest hadn't changed at all. Guiseppe Mastoni.

I blinked a few times to clear the fogginess, but Mastoni came to stand before me and asked, "Where is Reina Jaqulina?"

"What?" When I sat back, my shoulders pulled backwards, and when I felt the unrelenting plastic around my wrists, I realized I was zip-tied to a chair.

I barely registered the arm swinging for me before pain burst through my face and my mouth filled with blood. Spitting it out, I ran my tongue along my teeth and felt that one had loosened.

Why were they looking for Jax? It wasn't like she was hard to find.

Mastoni repeated his question, and I looked up at him. "I don't know where she is."

"You don't know where your own girlfriend is?" He crossed his arms over his chest in disbelief. When my eyes flicked to the woman in the corner, I saw that her foot was impatiently tapping on the ground.

"Look, I don't micromanage my woman. She is free to do what she wishes."

Reaching out, he backhanded me, and more blood pooled in my mouth. When he met my gaze, I spat it at him.

A blade quickly appeared in his hand and he lashed out, nicking my chest. I tried to hold back the hiss, but I was sure they heard it all the same.

"You seem to know an awful lot about me, but you don't know where Jax is?"

He flipped the blade, striking out near the side of my head, but I refused to move. Burning pain burst across my right ear, and then there was a flow of warmth down my neck.

Mastoni twirled the bloody blade in his hand before me as he bent down, his face flushed red in anger as he asked once again, "Where is Reina Jaqulina?"

"You know the definition of insanity is when you keep asking the same question over and over, thinking that there will be a different result. As for where Jax is, I really don't know the answer to that."

"It doesn't matter what you think or know. You are important to her," the woman from the corner said. There was something about her voice that was vaguely familiar. "She'll come for you."

"Unless you tell her to come and pick me up, how will she know where to get me?" Watching Mastoni pace back and forth before me, I continued, "Are you *really* sure I'm important enough to her that she would take time out of her day to come for me?"

An emotionless laugh came from the woman as she stood and the light hit her face. No, *fucking way.*

I'd seen that face on the news countless times. The slander, the mudslinging, the demands for Don McMally to return Jaqulina to her. I was speechless, but tried to hide my surprise.

Jax's mother stood, back ramrod straight and all arrogance, as she walked into the light so that I could see her better. "If I know one thing about my daughter, it's that she doesn't let just any man into the compound, into her home. If you were just a quick fuck, you never would have seen the inside of that house."

"You think you know her?" I stared down the woman who had treated her child like she was nothing more than a commodity to be traded or sold. My vision was starting to swim, and I shook my head to keep myself focused. "Think you know how she thinks? I think you put too much stock in what you remember of a child."

It was Mastoni who spoke next and started drilling me about the inner workings of the McMally business. I laughed, or at least I thought I had, because it was ludicrous to think that I would have even a crumb of that information. With every question I didn't answer, Mastoni continued to slice into my flesh, slowly and methodically, grinning at the blood that flowed from the wounds. I screamed when he went down my thigh. It was deep, and he looked me in the eye as he dug through the muscle. The pull of the zip ties on my wrists dug into the skin, and I could feel the blood flowing along my hands.

I vaguely remember hissing as he took a knife to my back. The physical pain was in the back of my mind as I reminded myself of what my grandfather had been through being in active duty during war time. I figured if he could get through that, this would be nothing to be able to have Jax in my arms again. From there on out, I didn't remember what else he did to my body. I just telling him I didn't know anything.

All I knew was that everything hurt, whether he was slicing with the knife or stomping on my feet over and over again, breaking the bones.

Everything came to a stop, though, when shots rang out on the floor above me. Mastoni stood and sighed, before walking out of the room. My vision was tunneling, but Jax's mother said, "I knew she would come for you."

Chapter Thirteen

Jax

As we cleared out the lobby of Needle Works and headed down the stairs, I paused for only a moment when I saw Guiseppe Mastoni slipping out the service door in the back.

"Fuck!" I checked my magazine, and ordered, "Check all the storage rooms. He's got to be here."

I kicked open the first door, and when I found it empty, I went back into the hall, hearing shots echoing through the space. Looking toward that end of the narrow passageway, I watched as one of my dad's guys, Bert, dropped to the ground.

"Reina Jaqulina," a voice I had tried to forget over the years sang out.

When the others froze and looked at the door, all the hate and anger I had kept bottled up over the years rushed to the surface. They instantly took position in front of me. I growled, and pushed in front of them, raised both of my guns and I turned the corner to see my mother with a gun at Cam's head. His eyes lifted to mine, and they held my gaze for a long, painful moment before they dropped as his head did. She grabbed him by the long, dark strands at the top of his scalp, pulled his head up, pressing the barrel to his temple.

"*There* is my daughter. God, you look hideous. I can't believe you would mar your perfect skin with all those other tattoos. Even if you do have the McMally raven over the back of your neck, it's disgusting." She lifted her head but remained hidden behind Cam. His eyes fluttered as he struggled to keep them open, and he was pale. Too *pale*. "And what did you do to your hair? I'm not sure what's worse, the cut or the color. You look like a boy, and not even a cute one."

Keeping my focus on her in case she so much as twitched to pull the trigger, I grit through my teeth, "It really is none of your fucking concern what I look like."

Cam moaned, and I took half a second to really look at what they had done to him. Rage and fear for him exploded through me, and my voice dropped, all my focus now narrowing on the woman who gave birth to me. "Back the fuck away before I put a bullet in your head."

"Not until you agree this one," she gestured to Cam before continuing, "goes in the river and to marry Dominic Mastoni."

A dark laugh came from my chest as I growled, "Not a fucking chance."

"This piece of rat shit is really worth the fight?" She pulled Cam's head to the side, and the gashes in his face and neck opened wider, encouraging more blood to flow down the side of him. "He's so beneath you. He will never understand your worth."

Rage built up to a dangerous level within me, and I saw my vision starting to fade from it. Slowly, I took a deep breath and concentrated on the fact that Cameron was still alive. He was breathing.

Look, his eyes just fluttered open.

He is actively bleeding.

Cam. I had to get Cam away from her.

Unable to get a clear shot to drop her to the ground, I aimed just to the left of her head, and squeezed the trigger. Cam hardly flinched as the sound rocketed through the room, but my mother jerked, let him go, and stepped a few paces away. Racing forward, I stepped around Cam, and positioned myself between her and where the man who held my heart sat, dying.

"Because you are my mother, I will give you one chance to put the gun down and leave. And that chance ends in ten seconds." I mentally started counting, and when her eyes narrowed, flicking between me and Cam. I wasn't even to five when she squared her shoulders, lifted the gun, and said, "You will be a Mastoni, Jaqulina. You will marry Dominic *tonight.*"

"My name is Jax McMally, and I will make my own decisions as to whom I marry." Those were the last words I said to her as I pulled the trigger. The bullet flew through the air and hit square in her chest. The woman who had called herself my mother looked at me with shock and confusion written all over her face. She swayed slightly, tilting her head to the side. Each time I pulled on the trigger, my chest loosened and I could breathe better. With each bullet, I watched as her eyes widened and the light faded from them.

She hadn't hit the ground before Alpha was cutting Cam loose. Turning toward him, I holstered my gun. When I reached out and cradled his head in my hands, blood coated every inch of my skin. "Cam, answer me, hun."

There was a light hum from him, and I leaned forward, gently kissing him before ordering against his lips, "Hold on. Doc will get you patched up."

As carefully as we could, Alpha team carried him upstairs, outside, and laid him in the back seat. When I climbed in, I rested his head on my lap and stroked his hair for the longest ten minutes of my life during the drive to the house where Doc was waiting.

When we came through the iron gates of the compound, I sat in the car as the guys went to get Doc. Jarvis however came around to the back seat and I helped him get Cam situated in his arms. Once we were set, we rushed him inside.

I couldn't think. I just kept clocking each slice, cut, and bruise. After the guys had Cam laid out on a bed in the garage, we pulled him into the elevator and made our way downstairs. Doc was waiting for us when the door opened, and he pulled him over to the surgery room.

Panic surged through me. "Surgery room?"

"It's just a precaution, Jax." Doc said as he and his assistant started cutting Cam's clothes off him. "We don't know what has been done with him, and there is a lot of blood."

I nodded. "Okay. Okay." I chewed on my thumb as I paced the back of the room, trying to give them enough room to work. I was so out of it, my brain didn't register anything they were saying. To be fair, I didn't realize how long I had been there until my father came down and wrapped his arms around me and I twisted into his chest.

"It's all my fault, Dad." I felt the tears falling, and didn't care that they were.

"It wasn't your fault, Jaxy." He kissed the top of my head and I continued to sob.

Dad moved us into the hallway where there a few chairs and sat us down. Pulling one of the chairs so that they were right next to each other, Dad held me until the tears ran out, and Doc came over.

I jumped up and Doc lifted his hands up in a wait motion. "He's going to be fine, Jax. There was some internal bleeding, but we got that fixed. His right foot is broken in six places, and all the toes are broken on the left. Otherwise, it's mostly superficial."

Relief washed through me, and I felt my dad squeeze my hand. "He's going to be okay?" Doc nodded. "Can I sit with him?"

"Go ahead." Dad said and kissed my temple.

I hurried into the room, and let out a long breath. He was hooked up to a bunch of machines, and I pulled a chair up next to him and held his hand.

I wasn't ashamed to admit that I sat there, watching his chest rise and fall. Wasn't ashamed that I was purposely shutting down my feelings and emotions so I didn't completely lose my shit. Mastoni and my mother had been working together. They abducted my Cam, and then they hurt him.

Doc worked relentlessly to make sure that Cam was okay. I double checked his vitals and when I took his hand in mine, I let out a long breath, letting it all sink in. Cam was hooked up to an IV, giving him fluids, pain medication, and an antibiotic.

I must have dozed in and out while sitting there. One moment, I was watching him with the lamppost light from the garden shining through the side window, and the next I felt fingers moving against my cheek and the room was bright from the sun.

I lifted my head, my throat tight around the single word, "Cam?" His eyes opened and closed a few times in slow motion, and tears rolled down my cheeks. "Oh my god, Cam."

His lips twitched, and he tried to open his mouth, but I leaned over him and kissed him softly. Barely pulling back, I muttered, "I was so scared. I never want to see you like that again. Fuck, I'm so sorry you got hurt because of me."

He huffed a laugh then groaned. I looked around, and my gaze met James's, who called for Doc. A moment later, he was standing at his bedside and giving Cam a few more painkillers.

"That should make you more comfortable, Mr. Martinez."

Cam nodded, and when his eyes met mine, he tried to lift his arm but I stopped him. "Don't move. You are pretty torn up." Pain shot through my chest as guilt threatened to overcome me again. "Damn it, this is all my fault. If it weren't for me, you wouldn't have been taken. Wouldn't be looking like you went through a cheese grater. I'm so sorry, Cam."

"Shhhh, baby." His words were rough and ragged, and it broke my heart.

"You are going to have a permanent shadow, Cameron Martinez."

"I don't need a shadow. This was a personal thing with your mom." He swallowed hard.

"You *do* need a shadow. You think I'm going to leave the man I love..." My eyes went wide as they met his. Shock went through me over the fact I'd said the words out loud, but I held his gaze.

"You love me?"

I smiled as the tears flowed down my face. "Yeah, Cam, I do. I love you so fucking much."

Wincing, he lifted his arm and cradled my cheek, wiping the tears. "I love you, too, Jax. I know that I may be overruled, but really, is a bodyguard needed?"

"I have to protect you." My voice broke at the words. Seeing him like that earlier tonight, knowing that he could stop my fragile heart from beating if breath stopped flowing from his lungs... that was a feeling I never thought I'd feel in my life. "Mastoni won't stop until he gets whatever it is he is after."

"You. He wants you," he said softly. "Can't really blame him. Have you seen yourself? You are stunning."

"Oh, I see the painkillers hit." I chuckled. "Seriously, Cam."

"I *am* serious. Mastoni kept asking where you were. I heard your mom through the fog of blood loss. They want you to marry the oldest."

"I can't marry Dominic when I'm going to marry you."

A bright smile crossed his face, and then sass filled his tone with, "Oh, is that so?"

"Yes. You are going to be Cameron McMally. No one will dare touch you. On top of that, I can have more of you every night."

He huffed a laugh and said, "You gonna ask me properly, or would you like me to do it?"

Smiling down at him, I threw some of that back. "I figure since you wanted some of the control in this relationship, you can handle that."

He chuckled a few times, but then it morphed into a moan. "Deal. Just need a few days to feel more like myself, okay, baby?"

"Deal. Now let me help you move over a little so I can snuggle up next to you."

"Jax..."

Looking over my shoulder, I hollared, "Doc!"

When he came into the room, he quickly checked Cameron's vitals, as he strode to his bedside. "What's wrong?"

I couldn't help but chuckle. "Nothing. I need help moving him over so I can curl up next to him.

"Jax–"

"I'm laying next to my boyfriend while he heals. Now, are you going to help me or not?"

Doc nodded his head and after a bit of careful maneuvering, he was moved over to the side enough that I could lay on my side next to him. Cam was panting a bit and had closed his eyes, breathing through the pain. Doc went over and pressed a button saying, "You'll be alright in a minute."

He glared at me, and nodded. I understood that I was the cause of his pain, but I was being too selfish at the moment.

"It's okay, Jax. Just let the meds kick in and it will be like nothing happened. Gently, I wrapped an arm around his stomach, careful not to touch his many bandaged wounds. He draped his arm around me, kissing the top of my head softly. His voice was groggy as he said, "Love you, baby."

He was asleep before I could kiss his side. "You too, Cam. I promise to keep you safe."

Chapter Fourteen

Jax

It had taken six months to dismantle Mastoni's business, realign his partners with us, and dismantle his empire. His wife had even left him when he lost all his capital. It was sad how easy it had been, but today was the day I ended the Mastoni reign.

As we pulled up to the hideout he had sequestered himself in, out in the middle of the forest, I chuckled. "Really? This is where he decided to hole up?"

"Well, you *have* destroyed his whole empire, Jax." Jesse said with a smirk.

I leaned my head back on the head rest. "It was almost too easy."

The old ratty cottage looked like it could hardly stand, and as Jarvis loaded extra magazines in the back seat, I kept my eyes trained on the structure.

Jesse was putting magazines in his belt when he looked down the road and sighed. "Why does this give me the feeling of a B movie that the second we get in range, the whole thing is going to blow up and will be lights out for us?"

Booker chuckled. "Because it does. Be aware of your surroundings. Boars are always wandering the hills here and saw on the news there was a monitored mountain lion making their way through the area."

"And we know that he's in there, right?" I turned to look at the boys in the back.

"Yes, ma'am." All three of them answered.

"Alright then." I opened the door, adjusted the small pack clipped to my belt, resecured a couple knives in my belt, pulled my gun, and slipped into the trees, with the guys right behind me.

We'd surveyed the property just yesterday with drones, scanning for any security features, and when we found none, we knew we needed to move fast. The fact a don was sitting out here so unprotected screamed that this was a trap. I had to end this. No one fucks with Cam. *No one fucks with the McMally's and lives.*

Looking in through the side window at the tree line, I saw Guiseppe, and his son, Dominic, Mastoni sitting at a little wooden table in the kitchen. Slowly, we made our way around the house, and when we got to the front door, I stood, gave a quick look to the guys, before striding up to the door, kicking it open.

Three guards were in the living room, and while we dispatched them quickly, by the time we turned to Guiseppe and Dominic, they had their guns up and were firing. Jesse cursed as blood sprayed from his shoulder and he dove behind one of the recliners.

"Dom, get out of here!" Guiseppe yelled at his son. The man turned, with hardly a backwards glance at his father, and headed for the doorway.

Spineless bastard. How dare you leave your father to die?

My finger squeezed on the trigger twice.

Dominic bolted through the door, and wood sprayed as the bullet hit the door frame.

Fuck! Booker ducked out back and took off after Dominic as I turned my gun on Guiseppe. To my surprise he only narrowed his eyes at me as I took a few steps toward him.

"Give it up. You're done. There is nothing left for you to go back to."

"No thanks to you." He pulled the trigger, and I ducked, but only a loud click filled the air quickly, followed by his curse. He racked the gun, but by that time I was already in motion, swinging at him. My fist landed right in the jaw, pain radiated up my arm at the impact, and I was a little surprised at how easily he lost his footing. I didn't wait, though, and kicked out with my entire leg, hitting him in the sternum. His gasp was music to my ears as he stumbled back and barely caught himself on the counter.

"Fucking bitch."

A smirk appeared on my face. "I am, but at least I'm respected, and still have my business flourishing." He was wiping blood from his mouth, and I took the moment to gloat. Gunshots rang through the air outside, and Jarvis slipped outside to help Booker. I glared at Mastoni, knowing that this was the end of his reign. "You. Have. Nothing. Not even a woman to warm your bed."

"You." He growled.

Laughing, I pulled a knife from my belt and played with it a moment, before flipping it in my hand and pointing the blade in his direction. "It was sad, really. You know what your wife did when I showed her how broke you were? She shrugged, and said that you always were a worthless loser."

The look on his face was one of horror and shock. "You really didn't think it was just the McMally's destroying everything you built, do you?" I threw my head back and laughed. "Oh, that's precious. No wonder Camelia was so eager to get out. You have no respect for women, do you? Your wife gave you a son, yet, you beat her whenever a deal went bad. *Of course*, she only stayed for the money. At least she had money, right? What are you without all that cash? Without all that so-called power you used to wield, Giuseppe?"

When he lunged for me, Jesse fired off three shots as I squeezed the trigger, hitting him in the shoulder, and Guiseppe fell to the ground. Rushing toward him, I kicked his gun further away, jammed or not. I wasn't taking the chance of him getting his hands on it again, and put my boot on his neck. Blood was flowing from multiple places in his stomach, and his breathing was labored as blood spread a crossed his chest.

"Get off me, woman!" Mastoni grabbed my ankle, but I pulled it from his grip, bent down, and plunged my knife into his heart. I stared down at his wide brown eyes, and twisted the knife between the ribs as I watched Guiseppe Mastoni stare off into noth-ingness. Once his body let out the last shuddering breath, I gripped the handle of the knife, and pulled it from his body, shaking the blood from the blade. There were a couple nicks in the blade, but I wiped off the blood on my jeans, and went to Jesse.

"You okay?"

He nodded, but leaned back against the wall in relief. "Thanks for keeping him occupied."

"Thanks for the cover." My attention was drawn out the door. Quickly, I changed out the magazine in my gun before looking at Jesse. "You good to move?"

He nodded, pulled himself up, and when we got outside, I stopped, turned in a circle, and tried to figure out which direction we needed to go. When I heard yelling in the distance, we took off through the treeline. We were about half way back to the SUV when I saw Jarvis and Booker with their hands on their hips, and looking up into a tree. Jesse stepped up next to Booker, who glared at his shoul-der. When I stopped, I stood next to them, and also looked up.

"Really, Dominic?" I was trying to slow my breath-ing, but I couldn't believe what I saw. There about twenty feet up the tree, Dominic Mastoni, was sitting on a tree branch, blood dripping from his leg and arm, but he was gripping his stomach so tight, I wasn't sure if the blood was from his arm or his gut. Looking at the trunk, there were a couple of broken branches, and the one just below the one he was sitting on, was broken with a bunch of blood on it.

A sly smile crossed Dominic's lips. "There is my soon to be wife. Call your goons off me."

"I'm a wife, just not yours, and no."

His eyes narrowed as I saw red creep up his neck, anger rising over him. "You did *not* marry that piece of shit Martinez, did you?"

"I know that you wouldn't be talking about Cameron like that, because then you would be disrespecting my husband, which would only make things worse for you. I'm also not sure why marrying someone would be a problem. It's not like I ever agreed to be *your* wife. Hell, you never even proposed. How badly could you have wanted me when you didn't even give me a ring?"

It was dead silent as I looked around. Not even the sounds of birds in the wind. There was something here. I scanned the area, but saw nothing. He shifted his weight. The branch creaked with the movement, and more blood dripped down, splattering on the leaves and dirt in front of us. Dominic's features hardened as he ground out, "You will be my wife. You were promised to me."

"If you think that my mother had the right to promise my hand to anyone, including yourself, you can think again."

"Your father will be dead soon, with no heir—"

Screaming, I fired off a shot. Smiling when his foot twitched and he let out a pained cry. "I *am* his heir."

He took a few labored breaths as he looked down and shouted, "No woman can be heir to a dynasty. That is why you are to marry me, and we can combine our reign. Maybe even take over the Don Supreme."

I scoffed. "If you think you can take over, you have completely lost all grip on reality. You can't believe I would have gone along with that plan, even if I *had* agreed to this side deal with my mother."

"You are a woman, and will obey me as your husband."

Before I could yet again rebut his statement, there was a blur of tawny fur, and a screech through the air as Dominic fell through the branches in the clutches of a mountain lion.

All of us jumped back further from the tree, freezing when the cat landed on the ground with Dominic, screaming for help, kicking and screaming.

"It must have smelled the blood." Jarvis said, trying to keep the panic from his voice.

Doing everything we could to not catch the attention of the almost seven foot long cat eating Dominic, we took large careful steps backwards. Its long lean body was free of marks except for a dark tipped tail that swished in the air. It was beautiful. One of the guys took my hand and pulled me backwards, but I tilted my head to the side, smiling as Dominic's gaze met mine. They pulled my hand again, and I continued to back up slowly.

Jesse's voice was panicked as he said, "Jax, we have to go."

I looked over my shoulder at them, and Jarvis dropped my hand, but I saw Jesse and Booker with their guns up and trained on the cat.

I suppose that would be a smart call. When I looked back at Dominic, I was half mesmerized by the cat's paw in Dominic's stomach, blood and who knows what else spraying everywhere.

Dominic's gaze met mine, and I gave him an evil smirk. His eyes widened just for that split of a second, before he realized I was going to let the giant cat have him. His screams became shrill as he tried to fight the animal off, but Dominic was already bleeding, his legs were not moving anymore, and the cat had him firmly in its clutches.

Taking a few steps back, I watched red spread across the fur of the animal and the way blood sprayed when it went for Dominic's throat, brought a smile to my face. The way the cat's claws shredded through him, as he screamed in pain, was extremely satisfying.

"Come on, Jax. Let's get you out of here." Booker's voice was low and careful as he pulled me closer to the vehicle.

Once we were safely back to the SUV, I slipped into the front passenger seat, and I heard the others take a deep breath, but I couldn't help shaking my head and start to chuckle. It quickly devolved into hysterical laughter as I thought about how the heir of a mafia don had just met his demise. "Not exactly how I envisioned this going, but not mad about the final results."

"Poor cat." Jarvis sighed as he pressed the button to start the engine. Still chuckling, I gave him a strange look. "Probably going to have indigestion from eating sour and rotten meat."

Jesse and Booker instantly laughed, with Jesse hissing at the end. Out of the corner of my eye I could see Booker in the driver's side back seat, turn to Jesse and sigh. "When are you going to learn that bullets are bad for you?"

The mischief in Booker's gaze had me looking at Jarvis, who chuckled. "Please tell me you've noticed them flirting the last couple of months." My eyes widened as I shook my head. "Yeah, let's just say that Jesse has had a bit of an awakening."

I watched them for a moment, and I could see it now. The way they were bantering with each other. The way that their gazes held a little too long.

"Good for them." I leaned back in the seat and let myself relax. "Jarvis, take me home, please."

"Yes, ma'am."

Chapter Fifteen

Jax

Epilogue

My fingers pressed down on the stencil, making sure it was smooth and set. Slowly, I removed the transfer paper, and after finishing getting everything prepped, I met Cam's eye.

"You ready?"

He gave me a sly smile. "Of course."

"There is no going back after this. You will be McMally."

He reached up and cupped my cheek. "I became a McMally the moment you put the first needle into my skin. Then again, when I signed paperwork, legally changing my name eight days ago. Not to mention that I plan on doing it all again in front of our family and friends in six months."

Leaning into his touch, I stared into his eyes. I knew all that to be true, but... My thoughts trailed off. "Being my husband is one thing, Cam. This is more."

"We've had this conversation, Jax. I'm not changing my mind, now get to it."

Cam's determined look morphed into something more lustful. It had my stomach tightening, and I ground out, "I swear, once I start, I'm not stopping, so if you want to fuck, I'll kick everyone out and ride you right here on the fucking table. So are we fucking, or am I putting this owl on your arm?"

He rolled his eyes and started playing a game on his phone. When I didn't start immediately, he gave me a sideways glance before looking down at where the stencil was placed, to the machine in my hand, and then me, raising an eyebrow.

"Alright, alright."

For two hours, Cam hardly flinched or moved, which was impressive. The underside of the biceps was a tender place, and most people found it a bit spicy. Only when I was done did he put his phone down and look back at me.

I leaned backwards over him, bent to stretch out my back, and when it popped, his chuckle rumbled through me. I relaxed as he made sure I didn't fall, but then his hand hit my core and rubbed.

"Cam." My voice was breathy as heat burst through me.

He chuckled, and helped push me back up. When I was up on my feet again, he sat up and placed his left hand out on the table. A moment later, I was placing the large 'J' and smaller 'ax' on his ring finger, and then putting the larger 'C' and smaller 'am' on mine.

I had just wiped off the last of the ink from my finger when both Jarvis, who was on guard duty with Jesse, and Cameron's phone's both went off. When Cam looked down at it, I was able to see it was the group thread with the girls. He tipped it so that I could read the message.

Bailey: Water just broke. Cam, tell Jarvis to get his ass over here, or he's sleeping in the hallway and I'll make sure he doesn't get to be there for the birth of his son.

I started chuckling, and looked at Jarvis. "You gonna check that phone of yours?"

His eyes were wide and Cam was smiling. "Get out of here. Jesse is here, and Cam and I will be along shortly."

Jarvis's phone rang then, and he answered it immediately. "I'm walking out the door, Sugar. The bag is in the car, and everything is ready to go. I'll be there to pick you up in ten minutes... Yes, dear."

With one last look behind him at us, there was true fear in that man's eyes.

About the Author

K.M. Ringer lives in California with her husband, little human, and two furballs, Wall-E (a Jack Russell mix) and Pippin (a Pomeranian Terrier mix). Always loving a little (or a lot) of spice she just might have you reaching for that "extra little help" to cool down.

Contact K.M. Ringer:

www.kimberlymringer.com

Instagram: @kimberlymringer

Facebook: Kimberly M. Ringer

Sign up for my newsletter on my website and receive freebies, coupon codes, and stay up to date on all things Kimberly M. Ringer and K.M. Ringer

Newsletter Signup

Ashes and Flame

ASHES
&
FLAME

KIMBERLY M. RINGER

After working as an Advisor for the Roman Empire, Tiberius Maximus Vispania returned to Herculaneum in 79AD to start over. When he meets Sidonia Regilla, a fire instantly ignites between them. She would be allowed to choose her future husband. Could Sidonia be happy with Tiberius?

Just when happiness finds a way, an epic tragedy occurs and the entire village is wiped out. Only Tiberius and his best friend survive, courtesy of a curse that's provided them with immortality.

2,000 years later, Kelsey walks into his bar and lights a desire within him that only Sidonia had ever done. When their dark worlds collide, an over-whelming need to protect her takes over, and he realizes there may be more to Kelsey's ability to get under his skin than he thought. When Kelsey is kidnapped and tortured, unknown old rivals and secrets come to light.

When Max rushes in to save her, he vows that either all of them would come out alive, or none of them.

WEEKEND SERIES

by K.M. RINGER

WEEKEND WITH RYLIE

Book One

Luci's whole life changes in one weekend with her boyfriend, Rylie Allen.

Of course, there was the mind-blowingly good sex. It always was, but then there are secrets revealed, and a new job opportunity that would change everything between Luci and Rylie. When her ex-boyfriend comes back to haunt her, it threatens to throw their lives into further upheaval.

WEEKEND WITH MALCOM
Book Two

Malcom Henderson has been obsessed with his Project Foreman for months. When she's disrespected at a bar he steps in and after an enjoyable night, he hopes to have it turn into something more. The next morning, she's convinced that as much as she wants him, it was only a one-night stand, and tries to protect herself by kicking him out. A torturous week pulls between them when unexpected problems are occurring on the job site that ends up being tied to the Chicago mafia families, and it's not long before Malk and Raquel find themselves in the middle of a brewing war.

WEEKEND WITH DESIREE

Book Three

With threats against the Don Supreme and his family lurking around every corner, Jensen Maloy, the most feared man in all Chicago, has been working overtime to ensure everyone stays safe and alive. Desiree Hernandez loves and trusts Jensen with every fiber of her being, and while she understands the reason, they need to live in lockdown, it doesn't mean she's happy about it. Even if she is living with her best friend and honorary sister, and her fiance.

Jensen and Desiree aren't used to being apart for such long stretches of time, and despite all the support from friends and coworkers, tensions rise, and morale drops to an all-time low. When the enemy takes drastic actions to finish the deal, they forget to factor in two very important things. Desi is not to be underestimated, and Jensen will stop at nothing to make sure his Princess is safe and in his arms. Who will still be standing when the dust settles?

WEEKEND WITH BETHANY

Book Four

Her strength will save them all.

Weekend with Bethany is the explosive conclusion to the Weekend Series. The war between Dallas and Vaux has become deadly, and no one is safe. When Beth is captured, she was shocked to learn that her Wes was the one and only Wesley Backnoff. Sure, she knew the name. Who didn't? Can she reconcile the compassionate man with whom she fell in love, with the killer who stands before her?

After rescuing Bethany, Wesley Backnoff, second to the Don Supreme of Chicago, can't hold back his feelings for her any longer and is bound and determined to keep her.

Old secrets come to light and threaten to destroy them all. Who will pay the price? Will Beth and Wes survive the night or has their time run out?

The Ashstrike Sanctorum

The Ashstrike Sanctorum:
Creation Story

When the Dark Witches of Moesia go rogue, and start creating immortals, will the paranormal creatures allow the new beings to live, or will they be out to destroy them? They have tasked Benjamin, an Ovexa, with finding three of these immortals to be interrogated to determine if they can be trusted to keep the paranormal world a secret from the humans.

Jorgen Hegland has found himself newly made but quickly learns being an immortal isn't worth it. When Benjamin finds him and demands he meet with the other creatures of the world, he agrees, but it isn't until he finds his mate, that he decides he will fight for his right to live.

The Astral's Bonded

The Ashstrike Sanctorum:

Book 1

Even Alphas have to answer to someone.

It was supposed to be a simple assignment. Astral Jade Romero was supposed to fix the werewolf problem at the Porter Ranch.

Only there was a problem, she hadn't prepared herself for, the human foreman Kolton Webster. He occupied all her thoughts and sucked her in like she never had been before.

When the wolves attack and Jade is injured will it be Kolton or the wolves that destroy her?

THE EXORCI'S TOUCH

THE ASHSTRIKE SANCTORUM:

BOOK 2

WHAT DO YOU DO WHEN YOUR ASSIGNMENT

DOESN'T DIE.

Exorci Jesse Westbrook can't touch anyone with his bare skin. If he does, they die. Such is the curse of an Exorci, the executioners for the Ashstrike Sanctorum.

His job is as simple and complicated as that. Receive the name and location of the person, and with a simple touch, the extermination is complete.

Jesse's life isn't all death and destruction. He has Maddie Taylor. The woman is his forever, but he's never dared to truly touch her. When her brother dies, her life spirals out of control, to the point she pushes Jesse from her life. Now... Now she's his next assignment.

<u>MY KISMOT SAVIOR</u>
<u>THE ASHSTRIKE SANCTORUM:</u>
<u>BOOK 2.5</u>

Angelica's life has been nothing but hiding from her parents and trying to make ends meet. It's been hard, but worth the freedom it afforded her from her family.

Morgan would have never guessed he would have found his queen just walking down the streets of Carmel, California, but there she was, arguing with the most despicable of women.

When Morgan intervenes, chaos ensues and Angelica and Morgan's secrets come to light quickly. Only Angelica seems to have one more...

<u>THE KISMOT'S UNDESIRABLE</u>
<u>THE ASHSTRIKE SANCTORUM:</u>
<u>BOOK 3</u>

Masen Cartwell was the son to the pride's king. It was his responsibility to ratify the treaty by marrying the Los Padres pride's undesirable, Veronica Aktins. There is something about her though. Something that pulls at his protective instincts and calls to his tom.

Ronni was the daughter of traders to her pride, an outcast, the Undesirable. Used and assaulted by the princes, the King has demanded that she marry the rival pride's prince and kill the Ventana Prides ruling family. Only, when she meets Prince Masen, his possessiveness over her and the adoration he showers her with sings to her heart.

When Prince Edwin steals Ronni, Masen will do anything to get her back. He had promised to protect her and keep her safe from her old pride.

Masen Cartwell won't let anything happen to what is his, and will stop at nothing to have his Queen back.

UNDER THE NEEDLE

MY KISMOT'S BELOVEDS
THE ASHSTRIKE SANCTORUM:
BOOK 3.5

Leo Banks has watched his best friend and his prince find their mates. As hand to the crown prince, he was okay with that. They found their happiness and now his princess, and a woman he considered a sister, was pregnant with twins. He vowed to be her protector through the troubled pregnancy. He was happy with just being Uncle Leo.

Then when her pregnancy takes a turn for the worse, Dr. Marie Fuller and her nurse, Hadrian Fuller, come to Landow to care for her. When they arrived, Leo was not expecting to find his mate, let alone a queen and tom.

Can he balance the stress of protecting his princess, and welcoming his mates into his life?

www.ingramcontent.com/pod-product-compliance
Lightning Source LLC
Chambersburg PA
CBHW030830200726
48285CB00007B/2402